KARI KILGORE

TEAM BUILDING REVENGE

Spiral Publishing, Ltd.

A Disagreeable Dinosaur Best Left Buried

When I turned back, three sliver-shaped ice cubes freezing my palm, Laura stood in the break room doorway.

An absolutely disgusted expression on her gorgeous face.

"You will never *believe* who I just saw in the hallway, Angie. Never. Talk about a Ghost of Bad Jobs Past."

"You're joking. You worked with him too?"

She shuddered, and the part of me that wasn't icked out with the sliminess of encountering Mike Billings perked up right away. Laura's thick honey-blonde hair shifted across her shoulders, and she rolled her huge blue eyes in a way that captured my grumpy GenX heart all over again.

"Unfortunately yes, I crossed paths with that jackass. Way back in the bad old days of the early Nineties, when women in IT were few and far between. I hadn't quite developed my current levels of Don't Give a Shit when it comes to guys like that, or maybe there just aren't as many of them around. Anyway, I'm sorry to say he knocked me for a pretty bad loop."

The Changes Cascade

Near Future Forward (with Jason A. Adams)

Dispatches from the Galaxy: A Space Opera Novella Trio

Dangerous Days on a Pleasure Planet

Storms of Future Past:

Dreaming the Storm

Joining the Storm

Into the Storm

Fighting the Storm

Storms of the Heart

Storms of Future Past Omnibus

Voices Through Time:

Songs in the Mountain

Secrets in the Land

Sorrows in the Earth

Walking the Ghosts

The Odd Society:

Independent by Means of Magic

Protected by Means of Magic

Collections:

Anthologies *with Jason A. Adams*:

For every woman (and man)
who ever had to grind out a smile at work

and daydreamed about turning the tables

Team Building Revenge

1

If there's one thing I've learned in my decades toiling in the information technology trenches all across Atlanta, it's that the break room is the beating heart of any organization.

Any organization worth its salt enough to have unlimited amounts of free, strong caffeine, of course. The preferred brain fuel for professional nerds the world over.

And the break room at my new gig has the good stuff as far as I'm concerned. Bags of fresh, perfectly roasted beans, and a gleaming, silvery object of worship in the form of an industrial-sized grinder to turn those beans into the raw materials for coffee.

The heavenly elixir I had on the brew worked its magic on my weary mind and body through smell alone, even before I brought out my tankard-sized mug.

As usual, I timed my arrival early enough to avoid the break room rush, and to give myself a chance to enjoy the red-tinged September morning outside the wall of windows. Here on the east side of Atlanta—and pretty much anywhere in Georgia once you get south of the mountains—we won't see a sign of autumn for a while yet. Not when it's still routinely in the eighties out there.

So the fifth-floor view's all green treetops with a few other plate-glass towers close by, and the much bigger towers of downtown Atlanta off in the distance, doing their best to blind me with reflected sunlight.

Yeah, I admit it. The vista is nice and all, but I'm here for the peace and quiet before I'm overrun with needy clients and their network security woes.

And to dump double the amount of ground coffee in the brewer's hopper before anyone can wander in to stop me. Tastes better that way, and gives me a premium solitary morning jolt.

We've only had to stage a bean resupply raid on accounting a couple of times since I've been here. I figure they'll get their ordering schedule sorted out soon enough.

The rest of the break room—aside from the all-important altar dedicated to high-end wake-up-juice machinery—fits the general twenty-teens corporate mold well enough. Plenty of little round white tables with matching chairs, comfortable enough for an ambitiously quick lunch or coffee break, but carefully engineered to put your ass to sleep if you're tempted to hang around longer than that.

Not one but *two* refrigerators the same stainless steel as the coffee apparatus, with printed signs warning everyone who dares glance that way to POLICE YOUR OWN LEFTOVERS and RESPECT YOUR TEAMMATES: DON'T POACH THEIR FOOD.

Sad state of affairs when adults need that kind of instruction right in their faces every day.

And I've been on the wrong end of too many disappearing sandwiches and accidentally knocked-over containers full of unidentified biohazardous material abandoned in a work fridge to dare argue. Not to mention a whole lot of the job description for IT really is code for, "You'd be amazed at how many adults either can't read the instructions or can't be bothered to try."

Anyway, I'm in too good a mood this morning to argue.

I not only successfully managed to dodge the *extremely* long weekend full of Corporate Team

Building Torment in the North Georgia mountains by making my daring escape last Friday.

Unnoticed and, so far, entirely un-scolded.

I also managed to bust my work-crush turned full-fledged girlfriend Laura out of there too. The whole insane adventure will hopefully make for a fabulous running-for-our-sanity origin story someday.

And let me just say we had a hell of a weekend celebrating our great escape.

Enough so that I couldn't be any more tired if I'd remained trapped in the land of endless rah-rahs and company spirit instead of cutting out of there faster than you can say Team Obstacle Course.

I only dropped her back at her place late last night. And spent the rest of the night wishing I'd gone inside with her.

So naturally when I heard someone walking in soft-soled shoes across the shiny white break room tiles behind me, I assumed that was my sweetie, sneaking in to wish me good morning.

I turned, big goofy smile on my face, and froze.

This was a guy, for one thing. A guy I'd never seen before, in this break room, during my pre-work alone time, or any other time.

A little taller than average, kind of rounded face with flyaway brown hair that was only going to keep retreating across his skull, but he had the good sense to let it do its thing rather than attempt a combover. The usual tan khakis/red golf shirt/brown loafers combo anyone who's ever made their way through the Corporate America Display of Lazy Fashion would recognize.

He seemed almost as surprised to see another human more-or-less functional as I was, but he managed a careful half smile, which was miles ahead of my locked-up-solid mind and mouth.

When I tried to catch my breath enough to at least attempt a standard-issue generic good morning, my lungs ceased all operations.

They caught on before my eyes and my brain that while I had no idea *what* this guy was doing in my break room, *who* he was presented a hell of a lot less of a mystery.

I *had* seen him before.

Worked with him before.

Quit a job with no concern whatsoever for the towering inferno of bridges I left behind to get away from him, which is *not* the way I tend to make a career change.

Not unless something—or someone—at said job did something to deserve it.

Mike Billings fit *that* bill better than anyone I've ever run across, and I've run across some Grade-A Prime IT Assholes in my years in the business.

None of that mattered anywhere near as much as finding out what the hell Asshole #1 was doing standing in *my* break room at *my* great new gig.

"Morning," he said, clearly unaware of the embers buried under years and several better jobs fanning themselves into a good and angry flame in my belly. "Sorry, didn't mean to interrupt. I'm usually the only one crazy enough to show up this early."

I managed to nod slowly enough that I heard my neck muscles creak.

"Yeah, sorry, morning to you, too. Getting an early start myself, just after some coffee."

He sauntered forward, going for one of the stupidly wasteful polystyrene cups beside the coffee machine, and throwing me face-first into a memory I'd rather have left in the depths.

Same Mike with a little more hair, standing in another break room on the north side of Atlanta. One hand on his hip, the other shaking a finger in a true sweetheart of an office manager's face.

Lecturing her about how ridiculous it was for him to have to bring in his own coffee cups just to appease some bleeding-heart environmentalist liberal bullshit.

The jackass never gave the office manager or anyone else the chance to point out how much money that saved the company, and how they'd put the investment back into a charity fund.

For the mercifully short time I worked there, Mike never tired of whining about the damn coffee cups. Not even when one of our co-workers got sick to death of hearing it and brought in a bag of the disposable kind to shut him up before someone strangled him.

"Smells like you're making rocket fuel there," he said, laughing. "Always did like a good strong brew. That and a company smart enough to avoid falling into that recycling nonsense. Not that there's anything wrong with *you* bringing in your own. We should have the choice is all, and we need good manufacturing jobs. This stuff is actually made of the byproducts of oil refining, you know, so the truth is these *are* recycling."

I closed my eyes and breathed in heavenly coffee-scented air that didn't calm me as much as it would have only a few short minutes before, then let it out as quietly as I could.

Yep, same guy.

Same argument.

Magically brought forward thirty years, fully intact from the mid-1990s.

He even spun the cup between his fingers the

same irritating way that made a squeak that set my teeth on edge.

Mike had somehow discovered a time machine, but one that only transported jerks.

"By all means, *ladies* first."

I looked up with my usual twinge at that word that I'd hated since my older relatives tormented me with it when I was a kid back in the 70s and 80s. They thought it was just so terribly *cute* that I wanted to be called young woman rather than young lady.

And the ones who were still kicking around the planet never let me forget it, even now that I was hardly a young *anything* in my mid-fifties.

Mike had absolutely wallowed in using that word, and never failed to add that same condescending sneer.

"Sure, thanks," I said, willing him to at least shut up if he couldn't vanish back into whatever toilet-shaped rip in the space-time continuum he'd excreted himself through.

I grabbed the polished steel carafe and loaded my tankard almost to the top, using half of the brew and not giving a damn. I stepped back to add my customary splash of creamer and one sugar, debating whether to grab my usual couple of ice cubes from the freezer.

I know, that's hardly standard around these parts, meaning in the US and in nerd-space. But scalding my mouth first thing in the morning has a nasty habit of putting me in a sour mood all day.

Not that I needed much help with that on this particular Monday.

"Save some for me, why dontcha?" Mike said in exactly the same fake boisterous tone I wished I could forget. That I *had* forgotten until today.

How had he escaped unscathed by time, fate, our changing society, or simply having a fed-up coworker knock his head against a balky server repeatedly until he stopped being annoying?

I decided to grab the ice after all and risk another of his pathetic little quips. Waiting for my mood-stabilizing drug of choice to cool to a drinkable temperature seemed like a terrible idea.

He turned before I could move, pouring a glug of creamer and following that up with three sugars to create a pale slurry that barely passed for coffee.

"Anyway, I'm Mike. Just started this morning, gonna do my best to wrangle the girls on the help desk into line. You know how it is, trying to get a bunch of the usual parade of warm bodies answering the phones to follow some kind of standards before they're out of a job and out the door."

2

Mike waited, eyebrows raised, obviously expecting me to fall right into the typical break room banter despite the fact that I'd barely said a word. If his social skills were as ossified as his points of view on recycling and using words like *ladies* and *girls*, he probably hadn't noticed me not speaking much.

In this case, getting it over with was the fastest way to get the hell away from him.

But all I could think was *Don't say Angie, Don't say Angie*, over and over again. Which of course made my shock-addled mind struggle to focus on anything besides my own first name.

The best I could manage to squeeze out was my middle name instead.

Not exactly original, I know. Disgust mixed with panic does that to the best of us.

"June. My name's June. Network security. Enjoy your day."

He blinked, and for a gut-wrenching second I thought he'd recognized me from all those years ago. I suppose it's possible. I hardly look like the kid a couple of years out of college I'd been back then.

Same wavy brown hair, just shorter now and shot through with a respectable amount of silver. Metal-framed nerd glasses instead of contacts after way too many years staring at way too many screens.

Still wearing my own version of generic corporate uniform, with black pants and a purple button-up shirt I'd chosen because I wanted to look cute for Laura.

I have no idea why I gave him my middle name, except that the idea of a stroll through the Gallery of Bad Jobs Better Left in the Past did *not* sound like my idea of fun.

He finally shrugged and held up his wasteful foam cup full of vaguely coffee-flavored sugar water.

"You have a good day too."

He strolled out again, not exactly whistling, not through his lips, but making an even more irritating noise by blowing across the roof of his mouth.

I put my tankard on the nearest table, and yes,

stomped over to the fridge. I'm not proud of it, but my feet did indeed strike the floor with considerably more force than necessary.

And it didn't even make me feel better.

When I turned back, three sliver-shaped ice cubes freezing my palm, Laura stood in the break room doorway.

An absolutely disgusted expression on her gorgeous face.

"You will never *believe* who I just saw in the hallway, Angie. Never. Talk about a Ghost of Bad Jobs Past."

"You're joking. You worked with him too?"

She shuddered, and the part of me that wasn't icked out with the sliminess of encountering Mike Billings perked up right away. Laura's thick honey-blonde hair shifted across her shoulders, and she rolled her huge blue eyes in a way that captured my grumpy GenX heart all over again.

"Unfortunately yes, I crossed paths with that jackass. Way back in the bad old days of the early Nineties, when women in IT were few and far between. I hadn't quite developed my current levels of Don't Give a Shit when it comes to guys like that, or maybe there just aren't as many of them around. Anyway, I'm sorry to say he knocked me for a pretty bad loop."

My chest tightened, and I had to fight back a powerful urge to cross the room and hug Laura tight. We'd both agreed over our amazing spending-every-minute-together weekend that keeping things on the quiet side at work was best, at least in the beginning. More to keep such a delicious secret to ourselves than for what anyone else would think.

Right now that felt like the worst idea ever hatched between two love-struck humans to me.

Partly because my next logical action would be to trot myself out of our calm, cozy break room and give Mike's head that long-overdue series of server-smacks myself.

Instead I dropped my half-melted ice cubes into my coffee and crossed the room to take Laura's appropriately huge coffee vessel from her hands.

"Leave room for creamer, right?" I said. "Anything I need to know about how Mike treated you while I'm formulating my grand plan for revenge? There's still time to tweak it toward the much more interesting and exciting side if necessary."

Laura grinned and I predictably went weak in the knees, but somehow managed to stop myself from kneeling before the caffeine altar.

"If *you* brewed the coffee, no need for creamer. I might try that ice trick, though." She walked up beside me, rubbing her hands together like she was about to feast on a particularly juicy carcass of jackass, roasted to perfection.

"Revenge, huh? Of the Angie-inspired kind? *That* I'm one-hundred-percent up for, Monday morning or not. As far as that jerk is concerned, he didn't do anything physical, or else I would have knocked him a good one and brought my friends in to finish him off. He's more the kind to do everything he can to undermine people's confidence and make them feel like they're in over their heads. If he couldn't manage that, he wasn't above getting us fired if he could."

"Sounds like he didn't vary his vile bullshit much," I said, handing her the not-quite-full vat of coffee. "He set his sights on me after I caught him changing folder permissions on other people's computers so he could snoop. Back in the long-ago days when Windows NT was cutting-edge and the world was fresh and new. My proof was too iron-clad for him to get rid of me. But I finally got sick of his bullshit and got rid of myself. Best career change I ever made."

Laura's laugh lightened the greasy gloom of that burst of rancid memory.

"I believe it!" she said. "I caught his ass snooping around in other people's email inboxes. Turned out he was every bit as ignorant about how Exchange and

Outlook worked as he was that we'd magically exited the 1950s and his patriarchal ideas about the workplace. I'm sorry to admit he circled the good-old-boy wagons fast enough to get me fired. Made a huge show of having me escorted out of the building as if I'd sold top-secret information on the remarkable amount of porn stashed on the firm's computers to their biggest competitor. Kinda wish I had."

"I suspect we're either avoiding or assuming a big part of the story here," I said. "Did you ever see or hear of him pulling this crap with men? I never did."

She grabbed her own ice from the fridge and slowly walked back toward me, shaking her head.

"Not once. And you're nowhere near the first woman I've talked to since who ran into his misogynistic reindeer games, either. Honestly, a few of us suspected he agitated to hire women just so he could run them through his heart-and-soul grinder. I was never sure whether he was actually trying to drive us out of the field or if he got off on it in some especially twisted way that I never want to know more about. The worst part is he *did* drive women out of the field. Several that I know of."

I leaned against one of the tables and sipped my coffee, breathing in the strong, earthy aroma.

"There were a bunch more of those knuckle-draggers around back then," I said. "Still too many now, but it's gotten better. They seem to have been yanked kicking and screaming into an era where *girls* not only dig computers and tech, no matter how much they might wish it wasn't so, but we're damn good at it. Listen, since he's made it this long, we may not be able to shove his antiquated ass out of IT, or even out of this place. But we might be able to get even and have a great time doing it."

Laura stood beside me, shoulder to shoulder, close enough that I could smell the citrus of her shampoo and her warm, clean skin underneath. We probably had a good half hour before anyone else wandered in, but with the earlier Unpleasant Surprise of the Jackass Kind, I managed to restrain myself.

"You know," she said, "there's quite a bit we can get done around here between the two of us. Once you're in charge of network security and email, the vengeful sky's the limit. And I'd bet we can each get in touch with some of Mike's other victims, too."

I leaned in for a risky and risqué peck on her soft cheek, and her low, sexy giggle made it all worthwhile no matter what happened.

"There are so many reasons we're a good match," I said. "And a dreadful one, if you're the kind to end up deserving our special attention. Let's see what we can't cook up, shall we?"

3

It's remarkable how quickly a plan comes together when it's on the diabolical side.

By the time Laura and I got back together that evening, we weren't meeting for the romantic reunion I'd been daydreaming about since I dropped her off at her house the night before.

Until work on The Plan really kicked in, that is, and my thoughts turned to a different sort of satisfaction.

The truth is I'd gotten so consumed with figuring out what we could get away with, and where, and how, and how many women Mike had pissed off over the years, that I didn't think about alone time with Laura nearly as much as I expected to.

Because when it came to Mike and his one-man campaign to keep the sacred testosterone-swamped culture of information technology pure, we were nowhere near alone, and getting less so with what felt like every passing minute.

Turned out a quick flurry of early morning emails and text messages from both of us got a startling number of replies. Then a continuing stream of updates as one woman got in touch with another woman who figured out how to find another. Each and every one of them enthusiastically on board with helping Macho Man Mike understand the many errors of his outdated ways.

Or at least having fun and getting a bit of long-overdue satisfaction in the process.

With a quick bit of rearranging from a dear friend of mine who owned a fabulous bar and restaurant in Decatur—and owed me a gigantic load of culinary favors for saving his business from sloppy tech security—Laura and I found ourselves in a big private dining room with twenty-three of our brand-new best friends.

Not the typical kind of room usually reserved for business meetings that you might be imagining, probably because this wasn't the usual sort of business.

My buddy Juan had more of an old-school geeky playground set up for those of us who remembered what an Atari was, and who'd spent an unhealthy amount of time scouring the shelves at Blockbuster looking for a VHS we hadn't already seen a dozen times.

Yes, I mean those of us born long before the World Wide Web and smartphones were even a gleam in a clever designer's eye.

Juan had created a doozy of a Generation-X playground.

The walls and ceiling were dark purple, the better to display movie and TV posters and such from the 70s, 80s, and 90s. He'd also brought in standup games and gaming systems from those glory days, or at least clever little machines capable of emulating them.

If we hadn't been so laser-focused on working out our nefarious plan for sweet, sweet revenge, we could have warmed up for dinner with hyper-competitive games of Space Invaders, Donkey Kong, Joust, BurgerTime, Moon Patrol, and my all-time favorite, Tempest.

Or we could have lounged on a wide variety of sofas—all either scratchy brown or green wool or that oddly slick velvet with flowers and birds all over it— aggravating our varying degrees of work-related wrist strain playing Atari, Nintendo, or Intellivision. Juan did break the spell a bit by bringing in flatscreen TVs rather than the ancient box versions.

Apparently the heat and power bill were worth

the detour from nostalgia overload, not to mention the never-ending struggle of keeping televisions that old in working order.

He'd even stocked board games from the era to go with a no-quarters-needed jukebox stuffed full of the best disco, Eighties and Nineties pop, and a refreshingly large selection of grunge and alternative from our young adult years.

And our early career years, when most of us had first encountered Mike and men a lot like him.

That long-ago mosh-pit soundtrack was exactly what played as we all gathered around several tables pushed together at the end of the room, far enough away from the vintage brown-toned carpets and area rugs to avoid unfortunate spills. After a sensible amount of time for introductions, chit-chat, and feeding our bellies, we stared at each other across decimated platters of fancified pizza rolls, gourmet mac-and-cheese bites, and high-end fish and chicken sticks with loads of unreasonably good dips.

Outspoken as I often am, I'm nowhere near comfortable with taking the lead in a group of strangers, much as people have tried to convince me to do just that over the years.

No, I *don't* want to lead a seminar about network security, thank you very much, or teach several tech types about the latest threats and safety protocols. I'll write articles or documentation about it for the right price, sure.

But standing up in front of a crowd? Without having had enough to drink to make karaoke temporarily sound like a great idea (again)?

Forget it.

And Laura once again won my heart by standing beside me, that gorgeous hair falling loose and free over the back of a decidedly non-work-appropriate black dress that hugged her in *all* the right places.

"So I'll jump right in since we all know why we're here, and how much we want to get started on the freaking killer food I can smell and see if it's as delicious as the appetizers we destroyed. We're all agreed that one man making it his mission to make women in tech miserable before we really even got started has earned our undivided attention. Especially now that we have the numbers and the power to do something about it. What kinds of ideas did y'all bring?"

I felt like a middle-aged frump in my own black t-shirt, black jeans combo that came straight out of the era resurrected all around us, but the dazzling smile Laura flashed my way as she sat made it clear I was *her* frump.

A cute red-head I didn't know piped up right away.

"The story of you two ditching the corporate cozy-cozy conference last week made you my new heroines. I say we set up a fake tech event of some kind and lure him in. Something his over-bloated ego can't resist. Then give him a generous helping of his own nasty medicine."

Edie McAdams, a fellow security geek who'd made the leap to graphic design, jumped in next. Despite her high levels of digital brilliance, as she spoke she scribbled furiously on an Analog Data Tracking Device.

Otherwise known as a spiral notebook.

"I got the invitations covered. He'll never know the difference, and no one else will, either. And I'm your woman for any kind of teeny tiny camera needs you might have, as long as I can get access to the venue a couple of days early."

"Good," I said, excitement overcoming shyness with record speed. Spite will do that for you. "What do we know about his background? What he's been doing all these years that we can use?"

Renee, a brilliant Black woman with a gorgeous set of spiky red and blue braids waved her forked pizza roll my way.

"He'll jump all over the chance at *any* kind of management. The slightest whisper sets his shriveled little heart aflutter. He's been chasing that impossible dream since the late Eighties, believe it or not. You'd think he'd get the damn clue after almost forty years, but not hardly. No one's fired him *directly* for being a sexist prick, but the personnel comments haven't been pretty all the way up until a couple of months ago." She shrugged. "I may have had a quick look at his backtrail this afternoon. Just one of those handy skill sets you pick up over the years."

The low chuckles and nods around the table made it clear she wasn't the only one in possession of the sorts of talents you almost never get to list on a résumé.

"He's in low-level management at our place," Laura said, nodding. "I thought taking over the entry level help desk was a weird career move for someone who's been in the field as long as he has, but sounds to me like he'd see that as the perfect gig. That group happens to be all women at the moment, and all out for their first career-level jobs. Not much supervision either, since we all expect turnover to be high. I get the feeling our hiring manager wanted to turn that trend around and train people to get promoted with us instead of leaving, then turned around and brought in exactly the wrong guy for the job."

Just to my right, a woman I'd known almost since my first cringeworthy encounter with our slimy target jumped in.

"So how about inviting him to a conference tailor-made for his ongoing interests?" Rosita said. "We'll set up the event we all could have used to recover from dealing with his ass, or to learn how to keep him from attacking us in the first place. Something like *Securing the Ladder: Nurturing the Next Generation of Women in Information Technology.* Just enough corporate-feel-good nonsense to be believable."

"I like it," Laura said, beaming. "From what I remember, Mike is easily flattered enough to fall right through this trap door without much convincing. I expect once we put our proposal together with all the fabulous props and bells and whistles, pretty much anyone would fall for it."

"Only one suggestion," I said, thinking of Mike's Manly Monologue when I was too shocked by his appearance in the break room to respond. "Change it to ladies instead of women. He'd like girls even more, but even I can see that might be going too far. And if we need extra help or Juan's too booked solid to accommodate us, Laura and I know a badass culinary student who could use a short-term gig before she starts her last year of school."

Laura pulled me close with one arm and laid a big kiss on me, apparently not the least bit worried about keeping things quiet now that we were away from work. Not that I minded myself.

"Now *that* is a brilliant idea," she said, and we all turned to see a swarm of servers bearing food too distracting for our conversation to continue. "I get the feeling the self-appointed savior of nerd masculinity across Atlanta is about to harvest a few decades' worth of his own stinky karma. And I'm one hundred percent here for it."

4

The next couple of weeks passed in a dizzying blur of planning, excitement, spending as much private time with Laura as I could manage, and thanking my previous self for working so damn hard to make my job so easy to put on autopilot.

One of the best signs of doing something like network security right is when things pretty much run themselves. And that more-often-than-not routine of easily monitored stasis is exactly what they pay me for, whether they realize it or not.

The invitations and even a website our new friend Edie set up were indistinguishable from the hundreds I'd sorted through during my career. The brilliant touch of heavy ivory cardstock and glossy four-color brochures put the whole thing over the top, to the point that I almost wished the Securing the Ladder conference was the real deal.

Maybe I'd take that on as my next project to make up for my evil machinations on this one.

As far as Mike or anyone else receiving the beautifully designed and coordinated package could tell, they'd be attending an exclusive weekend retreat for a select few expert-level professionals, with an intensive focus on encouraging the women's talent pool for the future.

I would have happily bet the seriously overpowered espresso machine I had at home—a professional model that followed me home from a coffee shop going out of business—that no one outside our hyperfocused group would see anything out of the ordinary. Just another corporate-friendly design with rows of mostly faceless, cartoonish women starting straight ahead. Beautifully designed, mind you, but sure to get approved by the pickiest HR department in the land.

But between Edie's supremely capable hands and our shared nefarious intent, that inoffensive, under-the-radar design transformed into something more...focused.

Determined.

Maybe even menacing.

Our rescuer from All Things Corporate-Team-

Building stepped up without hesitation as well. Millie set up the use of a soon-to-be-renovated shelter from the same North Georgia Mountain resort she'd helped Laura and me flee from, along with fantastic photos for the brochures and a group of her fellow culinary students and a few pros to set up fake catering.

I wish I could say I was surprised so many women in *that* line of work were all too happy to help see at least one of the No Girls Allowed gatekeepers put in his place.

Laura handled the emails from our training department, suggesting Mike attend to "support his already stellar record of mentoring young professionals in our field." She also won the betting pool between all the women involved about how long it would take Mike to respond with his intention to attend.

I'd given him the generous estimate of four hours, probably because I'd scorched the earth behind me after running afoul of him all those years ago. Laura's far more unpleasant experience had her accurately clocking him at twenty-seven minutes.

We even got the quick cooperation of quite a few friends and partners and husbands of the male persuasion, to make sure Mike didn't walk toward a sea of angry female faces and bolt before the fun got started.

Edie's best friend Edgar was especially generous, and agreed to play along by standing in as the leader of our fictitious conference.

I'm here to tell you *no one* can resist Edgar's buttery rich I'm-the-trusted-authority-you've-been-waiting-for voice on the other end of a phone. So of course he took the time to record the voicemail greeting on the burner phone we bought for the occasion in case Mike decided to check in.

You know, to offer his extra-special bad advice services, maybe as a prize to the most deserving young woman making the questionable choice to get into our crazy line of work.

He did call not long after accepting our invitation —and returning his signed agreement to *all* of our attorney-designed, fiendish conditions of attendance —but only to verify what time he should get there, and whether he'd be expected to present or not.

Edgar reassured him that plenty of time would be set aside for their guest with by *far* the most experience of the topic at hand.

If Mike ever suspected a thing, he kept it to himself better than all the actors in Hollywood during a *good* year. He simply arrived early each day, interrupting my alone time with the gleaming metal caffeine goddess, and doing that annoying half-whistle thing everywhere he went.

If anything, he was a touch more smug than usual, which meant he took his most prominent personality trait to truly superhuman levels.

Laura and I did our best to keep an eye on the "girls" at the help desk to keep Mike from doing them too much damage, and Edgar had altogether too much fun sending enough updates about the exclusive event to hopefully keep Mike from his favorite tormenting target.

Through it all, the best part was waking up beside Laura every morning, and giggling to myself about what my life had become.

This amazing woman, a bunch of fantastic new friends, and spending my days plotting revenge?

What could possibly go wrong?

Which is the biggest mistake any member of our generation ever makes, even well into our middle age.

Asking that damn question, even in the privacy our own minds.

That Friday, when we were all set to drive up to the mountains to check out the setup and handle any last-minute details, my well-mannered network did what *all* networks do. Without fail, with the exquisite sense of timing that can only be achieved by non-sentient patterns of zeros and ones racing through miles of fiber-optic cable.

A vile new attacker—probably another bunch of zeros and ones—found an exploitable gap in my latest security wall.

And I was caught in the wrong place at the wrong time. Meaning halfway out the door, in time to beat the epic disaster of Friday afternoon Atlanta traffic, but still reachable.

By the time Laura tracked me down, I was already neck-deep in code and firewalls, and halfway to banging my own head against a server.

She looked strangely ethereal in the dim room, with all those red and green lights reflecting in her hair. And with the most calm and understanding smile on her face.

Which made me feel worse when I already felt like a dog turd ground into a brand-new wall-to-wall white carpet.

"You know the whole thing doesn't really start until tomorrow, right?" she said, stepping behind me with her arms around my waist.

Yeah, we sort of ditched the quiet-at-work thing along the way, too.

"I know, I just hate dumping all this last-minute crap on everyone else. But this server is already overwhelmed, and if it goes down, the cascade of shit will not be pretty."

"And no one else could possibly do a better job of taking care of this than you, Angie. While we've already assembled quite the impressive team of experts to handle getting ready for our Very Incapable Pig tomorrow. We've got it under control."

I turned to give her a proper hug, mainly to soothe my own disappointment.

I never did say I was especially noble.

"If I get this wrapped up faster than I expect, I'll be right behind you."

She laughed and shook her head.

"And dive headfirst into this traffic if you don't have to? At least wait that part of it out. But I'd say we'll have everything under control before then. If we do, and I can get to somewhere with cellular service, I'll let you know. There have to be working phones out there somewhere. They just keep them hidden from the poor fools dragged up there for corporate torment events."

"You mean people like us."

"Not like us at all. Thanks to you, we busted out of there, remember? And we're going back on our own terms this time. Good luck with your security breach."

I sighed, already envisioning spending a very

long, very lonely night that absolutely would not be worth the comp time I'd earn.

Not if I missed the revenge of our still-young century.

Barely an hour later, when I decided the problem was severe enough to require more of my extra-strength brew, the whole Mike-and-young-women-in-IT situation took more of a turn for the worse than even I expected.

I wandered into the break room, still squinting and blinking like an especially grouchy middle-aged bear rudely awakened from hibernation by the bright lights, and flipped them off as I passed through the door.

Self-preservation kicked in, along with a good dose of not wanting to actually bite an innocent co-worker's head off.

So much cleanup, even with the tiled floor. Anyway, who knows what you might catch from a human these days?

So I staggered toward the soothing blue glow of the coffee deity, muttering to myself about my next steps in restoring my violated firewall, cleaning up the mess, and steps for prevention of this particular disaster in the future.

Completely oblivious that I had company until I heard a furtive sniff from the side.

I demonstrated my already high levels of over-stimulation by jumping and letting loose with an undignified squawk. (Nothing at all like a bear, sadly. More like a goosed chicken.)

The room was lit enough for my brain-juicing purposes by the early September evening sun, but that light came from the wrong side of the building. Leaving shadowy corners around the edges of the break room, plenty deep enough to conceal whatever the hell was lurking there to startle my now-shaky ass.

My response was as clever as my squawk was intimidating.

"Hello?"

"Hi there," a small, trembly voice said. "I'm sorry for scaring you."

I considered pretending for a second, perhaps strutting over to grind my much-needed coffee beans with a flourish and turning with hands proudly jammed onto my hips to declare that I was the furthest thing possible from scared that anyone could be.

Striking a geeky superhero pose, if you will, along with a solid dose of denial.

Performing the age-old dance of the jaded old mentor setting an impossible example for the potential mentee to follow.

But something about that voice pushed me to be my goofy, grumpy, less-than-super self instead.

"No worries. Just my network-headache-induced jumpiness. Rough night ahead. I think *I'm* the one who interrupted *you*. Want the light back on?"

A soft, watery sigh, and I heard the metal legs of the chair scoot across the tiles.

"No, I'm okay now," she said in a much bigger voice. "I needed a break after all those phone calls this afternoon. Get the breach secured?"

5

I blinked as a woman stepped out of the dim corner, clutching a much smaller version of my stainless-steel tankard. The Newbie model, since she was clearly too young to have built up my rather impressive caffeine tolerance levels. Chin-length black hair that flowed like a waterfall when she moved her head, big brown eyes tilted up at the corners.

Unless my memory had taken a bigger hit than I thought from all the excitement of the past few weeks—and the stress of the past few hours—she was one of our fairly new hires for the frontline help desk. Probably just out of college, like I'd been when I jumped headfirst into the information technology river and never did manage to claw myself back out.

And I had a sick, guilty twist in my gut that I knew exactly what had her so upset.

It likely had a distinctly unpleasant Mike shape and stink to it. One we hadn't kept distracted nearly as well as we thought.

A Mike-shaped notification that called the breach in as if he'd caught it himself.

"Got it secured, yeah. Partly thanks to getting a quick notification. Are you the one who noticed it?"

She smiled and nodded, and the motion sent a getaway tear down her smooth cheek that she swiped away. Which I of course totally ignored, because I have yet to meet a woman who wants that kind of work-induced tear pointed out, especially if it's the angry variety.

"That was me. I've been taking online courses in network security as I have time, so I had an idea what was going on with the first calls." She looked away and rubbed her shoulder. "Well, I *was* taking classes. You know how it is."

I breathed as slowly as I could before replying. No need to scare this poor kid off by saying the wrong thing to her, and in the wrong pissed off tone, when I'd soon get the chance to say it to the guy who'd earned it.

"I *do* know how it is, but probably not the way you think. I'm Angie, by the way. Need more coffee, or tea? This time of night it's way better to brew fresh than risk getting a mouthful of overcooked tar."

"I know who you are, and I'm glad to meet you. I'm Tia." She shook her mini-tankard and nodded. "I could use more, sure. I'm on for another four hours."

"Mind if I use a double-grind? It's not all that much stronger, but it tastes a heck of a lot better."

Tia smiled, and my heart broke into a hundred memory-shaped pieces. I knew the smile of a woman who'd been treated like shit and appreciated the smallest kindness more than I wanted to admit.

I'd seen it in the mirror way too many times at that long-ago job I'd stormed out of.

"Double-grind sounds great."

"Then watch and learn, Tia, and we'll have a chat about network security, job security, and most important of all, staying sane in this career and in a place like this."

She let out a low, disgusted laugh, but she did sit.

I busied myself keeping my temper under control, starting a fresh pot, and rinsing the old one out for the weekend crew, in that order.

Before the last couple of minutes, I would have sworn on a stack of fresh extra-black t-shirts that the most important thing to me was wrapping up my network fix so I could head north.

But seeing Tia's face combined with the

reporting credit on the breach reminded me what the whole revenge scheme was about in the first place.

"Okay," I said, sitting across from her. "You have permission to tell me I'm full of shit and to back off, and I hope you will if that's the case. Just let me mention that I've been in this tech game since the early 90s, so I know the kind of nonsense that goes on more than you might think. I have the feeling something happened tonight that has you saying you don't want to take classes anymore. Which seems kind of strange to me, since you caught a tricky breach before it could do any real damage. And before anyone else, including me, had a clue. Thank you for that, by the way."

Tia brushed her amazing hair back, and it flowed perfectly back into place.

"You're not full of shit, and you're welcome." She smiled again, but only for a second. "I'm not sure... To tell you the truth, Angie, I'm not sure how much I should be saying to someone in management, you know?"

I snorted, reminding myself this youngster likely hadn't worked with many of my kind yet.

You know, grouchy, anti-social, tending toward cynical, and not even a little bit trusting of authority. Not even when we're dragged *into* authority, often kicking and screaming the whole way.

Typical for my generation, in other words.

"I can't tell you how weird it sounds for someone to call me management. Listen, I'll go first, or at least I'll be more direct. I'm concerned about changes around the help desk lately, and I'm not the only one. Did someone say something to you to get you upset?"

This time Tia leaned forward, elbows on the table, forehead in her hands.

"You could say that," she said to the table, but loud enough for me to hear. "I know I need to toughen up for this job, for *any* job. I guess I'm just not there yet. There were...quite a few questions about whether I understood what I was seeing, or if it was a lucky guess."

I nodded, rubbing my chin. Thankfully the brew cycle finished then, and I took my excuse to get up and turn away.

Keeping my expression neutral was no longer an option.

Two of the women Laura and I met at Juan's place for dinner had the same experience with Mike Billings, at different jobs. Both were going for in-house promotions, and because some higher-up either didn't care, felt the same about women in tech as he did, or was unreasonably optimistic, Mike was one of the hiring interviewers.

With each of them, he'd put them through all

kinds of hell with rapid-fire questions way above what the job called for, getting more and more impatient and dismissive no matter how they answered.

Then he'd wrapped his little game up by accusing both of them of lying on their résumés since they obviously weren't qualified. Not only for the promotion, but the jobs they already had.

One of them told him to go to hell and walked out and never went back.

The other put up with it long enough to get a different job, with Mike questioning her skills the whole time, often right in front of her and always with a crowd of witnesses.

I filled my tankard, dosed it with cream, sugar, and ice, then took the carafe to the table. When Tia looked confused and tried to reach for it, I smiled.

"I got it. And I'm going to take a guess now, but it's hardly random. Was it suggested you couldn't possibly be qualified or experienced enough to know what you were seeing? And not in the most polite of terms?"

Tia twisted the lid off her adorable little Newbie tankard and scooted it across the table with a smile more bitter than the sludge I'd rinsed out.

"Got it in one. So it's not just me, huh?"

"Not even close. Need room for cream and sugar?"

"Nope, straight up for me, especially as fantastic as that smells. I know I'm new at all this, and I'm here to learn. I get that. But I don't understand *what* I'm supposed to learn by someone talking to me that way, as if I've never seen a computer or even a screen in my life."

I filled her up and sat back down, watching her carefully twist the lid back on.

"Nothing worth learning," I said, "except that the people in charge can be insecure assholes sometimes. Would it help if I told you I had the same experience with the same asshole when I was around your age?"

"I don't know it if helps to know he's been pulling that shit for so damn long." Her eyes widened. "No offense, I didn't mean to say *you* were..."

I waved one hand and took a long drink of my heavenly brew.

"No one's going to mistake me for a fresh face, so don't give it another thought. And yes, I've recently discovered he's made kind of a shadow career of making women feel like crap. Drove more than one out of the field altogether. Often by doing things like trying to make a woman feel like dirt, claiming credit for something she did, and heading home early for the weekend."

Tia started to take a drink, then slammed her

tankard down hard enough that the coffee sloshed inside, spilling a bit across the clear plastic lid.

"I *knew* he was going to say he spotted the breach by that smug fucking smile. Why the hell did they *hire* him? We're all women on the help desk here, supposedly to help get more of us started in IT, and they bring in a jackass like that? Are they trying to weed us out through trial by fire or something?"

"I wondered the same thing myself when he came strolling in here a couple of weeks ago. Not the best way to start the week, with a hardcore flashback to the worst job I ever had. From what we can figure out, he's the one actually faking his damn résumé now. Or at least leaving more than one position off of it, probably to avoid anyone making those reference calls."

Tia blew out through her lips, then got that drink of coffee. It seemed to settle her agitation the same way it did for me.

If she made it through this rotten episode—and still wanted the job—I had the feeling she'd go far in this crazy line of work.

"*We* can figure out? There's more than you and me?"

I stared out the window at the darkening sky, and the orange glow of Atlanta coming to life. Wondering if Tia was ready to get dragged into our lively game of Getting Even, Professional Female Nerd Style.

"There are so many more, Tia. You have no idea. This is going to sound even stranger than what we've just been talking about, but are you busy tomorrow? A whole bunch of us who've known Mike way better than anyone should have to are planning a little revenge party in the mountains. At the same retreat center the whole company got dragged to a few weeks back. We've got room for one more if you're up for it."

Tia sat forward and opened her mouth, then closed it and took a deep breath. Then a slow sip of coffee while she watched me. I didn't have to be huddled there with a younger version of myself to recognize how much was going on behind her eyes right then.

All I could do was hope I passed the "can I possibly trust you?" exam I was sitting for.

"Other women who work here?" she finally said.

"Only one. Laura Alderson."

Tia nodded. "From the messaging group. Head engineer, email and mobile devices, right?"

"That's her." I ignored all the amazing things I could add about Laura, and the way my cheeks were probably red enough to be visible in the low light. "Other than that, these are women who've...encountered him before from all over the city. Going back to my vintage, and unfortunately several a lot more recent. You'd be the most current."

"You mean the only one who works with him right now," Tia said. "And since I'm pretty new and have no seniority or influence or much experience at all, I could lose the most by letting him know what I think."

"That's absolutely right, and you're damn smart to keep that in mind. So, if you do decide to go, feel free to hang back. We've got plenty planned for him, don't worry. And I'm not going to think badly of you one little bit if you flat-out don't want to deal with that asshole on a Saturday. The only reason I'm willing to is because I know just how richly he deserves everything he's got coming."

Tia pressed her lips together and nodded, still watching me.

"Okay. Can't say I enjoyed my wasted weekend up there even one little bit, but I'm in. I'll decide how much I want to participate when the time comes. Make sense?"

"One hundred percent. I promise this won't be nearly the exercise in corporate torment as the company retreat was."

We both got to our feet, hopefully with enough

caffeine and conversation to get through the rest of the evening. Tia flashed an honest smile for a second.

"This might be none of my business, but you weren't... I don't remember seeing you at that retreat. I would have, too, because I meant to ask you a few questions about network security if you'd let me. Did I just miss you?"

I laughed, realizing I was likely in the presence of another IT-lifer. Once she learned the tricks of dealing the likes of Mike Billings, of course. If any of us were lucky, there'd be fewer and fewer of his particular kind of dinosaur to deal with over time anyway.

The world did indeed move on.

"Well, I *was* there," I said as we walked out. "For a rather brief time that appears to have gone undetected by management, so it's no wonder you missed me. If you want to catch a ride up north with me after your shift, I'd be happy to answer those questions you had and tell you all about it."

This time Tia's grin brought her all the way back to the youthful exuberance she should have.

"You're on."

6

I hate to admit this, but it took me all the way until we got to the resort to realize just how brave Tia actually was to take me up on my offer.

All the rest of us had decades in the industry, or at least decades of work experience in some field or other. And the simple fact that we all knew each other after the rush of planning our festival of revenge made a difference too.

Tia, on the other hand, was on her first job out of college, still in her early twenties, and had spoken to me more than anyone else who'd be there, and that only for a few hours.

And yet she willingly ran home and packed an overnight bag, then rode with me for a couple of hours, then settled into one of our overly crowded cabins for the night.

Shows just how determined and courageous she truly was, even if she didn't know it yet.

Also shows exactly how badly a jackass like Mike affected her in just a couple of weeks.

If any of us needed convincing that our efforts needed to be worth it—or actually that they already would be—seeing Tia's response to being in a big group of women who understood and supported her more than did the job. She absolutely glowed at breakfast, like a big kid waking up to find Santa had loaded the living room up in spectacular fashion while everyone snoozed.

Our buddy Millie, who'd happily helped us escape the weekend of company sanctioned hell that Tia had endured, set us up in remarkable style.

The shelter she'd snagged for us was perfection, even if it was nowhere near as fancy or huge as the one the company had arranged with their much-larger budget. This one was the same high-ceilinged redwood construction, but only big enough to seat about forty rather than a couple hundred.

The shiny concrete floor had seen better days, with a few cracks here and there, and a few more stains I had no desire to learn more about. And yeah, the fireplace needed fresh mortar, and the little satellite kitchen lacked any sort of refrigeration or propane cooktops.

The upcoming remodel would undoubtedly leave everything looking brand new and up to the most anal city corporate standards for rustic, but not *that* rustic.

But the row of red brick grills would do nicely for our purposes, and all Millie's culinary school friends came equipped with huge coolers that would last more than long enough in the chilly morning air.

She'd brought several herself, tucked into the bed of her sunshine on wheels most-adorable-vehicle-*ever*, which the less imaginative among us might mistake for a cheery yellow mid-size Chevy pickup. But exactly none of us besides me and Laura had seen one quipped with huge curving eyelashes around the headlights, an irresistible image of pink, puckering lips on the front license plate bracket, and a pair of absolutely precious dangly pink earrings hanging from both side mirrors.

Sunshine. On. Wheels.

The truth was none of us thought we'd have to pull off a flawless recreation of corporate-rah-rah-team-spirit-building obnoxiousness, even though most of us had more than enough experience to fool even the most dedicated facilitator of group cheers and borderline-terrifying enthusiasm.

Mike had done most of the work for us.

Besides living up to his fragile-yet-monstrous

ego's history of bad behavior, he'd driven poor Laura and our convention recruiter stand-in Edgar insane with suggestions, questions, and badly disguised pleas for reassurance over the last few days.

My fears Mike wouldn't be able to maintain his relative quiet as the day grew closer proved pitifully true. Over the last couple of days, Laura's fake email account had fielded dozens of messages, while Edgar's burner phone rattled itself off the metaphorical hook with voice mail.

Verifying the location. Offering to review the retreat's programming, or coach the presenters on how to properly mentor the *fairer sex.*

Yes, he did indeed use that term.

Repeatedly.

Suggestions for catering. Queries about the background music, with lists of his own in case the search for properly inspiring tunes and cheers and chants proved too difficult.

Ideas for team building and networking. Helpful tips on how to manage the youthful lady's too-high expectations for future salary increases and promotions.

Edgar handled all of those return calls and text messages with far more charm and grace than any of the women who'd run across Mike during their careers could have managed.

I have no clue how he did it, but Edgar somehow managed to find the whole thing amusing.

Despite the painfully early, ass-crack-of-dawn hour of seven o'clock, our revenge-minded group gathered in a remarkably perky mood. The deep-blue sky and drifts of perfect little cotton-ball clouds combined with the treat of low humidity and a pleasant chill to the breeze, making the crime of being awake so early on a Saturday tolerable.

Millie and her friends helped immensely by providing an utterly sublime breakfast.

Whole-wheat blueberry pancakes that didn't need a scrap of butter or maple syrup but had plenty of both, to go with an omelet bar that would be the envy of any big hotel in the city. Four kinds of cheese, all kinds of fresh veggies, and a decadent selection of meat for those who wanted it. They even supplied the best-looking tofu scramble option I've ever seen, and Tia raved about how good it was.

I myself would swear they had to have extra-pampered and exotic chickens stashed away just out of sight for the eggs themselves to be so damn fresh and good.

It probably goes without saying that Millie and company brought copious amounts of coffee, tea, juice, and soda to leave us wide awake and absolutely spoiled for choices before the day ever got started.

Millie herself pulled me and Laura aside before the festivities got rolling—her curly brunette hair in an especially bouncy ponytail right on top of her head—to give us a sneak peek of the snack options for our mid-morning break and fill us in on their nefarious lunch plans.

Let me just say the best purveyors of brunch in all of Atlanta would have wept with joy at the wonders we beheld, and would soon inhale after the rush of all our vengeful plans falling into place.

The only question was whether Mike would hold out long enough to enjoy any of it, or whether he would flee before Millie busted out the extra caffeine, carbs, and sugar needed to sustain any business meeting worth its salt.

As has too often been the case during my career, I'd been drafted as the faux-leader for the day's merriments. I firmly believe it's because I'm too nice to say no, much less *hell* no.

And in this case, everyone else pounced on my more-or-less civil encounter with Mike in the break room. The unpleasant surprise that set all this into motion.

He'd make the mistake of trusting me if I was the one up front making introductions.

So after we'd stuffed ourselves with enough to

fuel the day and topped it off with our liquid rocket juice of choice, I faced them all.

A loose circle of more than fifty women, and the quiet support of about twenty of the *best* kinds of guys sprinkled in.

Each and every woman with some kind of mental or emotional scar from dealing with Mike, usually early on in her career. From me and Laura back in the Wild West days of the 1990s all the way to Tia with her much fresher humiliation.

And the ones like Millie and Edie—who'd printed up a first-rate stack of folders and name badges and her beloved spiral-bound Analog Data Tracking Devices to make the whole event even more official-like—had known way more than their fair share of men like that.

Sometimes women, absolutely. I myself went straight from Mike's bullshit to a female manager who turned the abusive workplace spigot up to eleven and worse. She not only played the humiliation game like a legendary Vegas hustler, but she amped things up to virtuoso by playing our team against each other rather than doing all the dirty work herself.

The thing about her, though, was she was an equal-opportunity oppressor. No difference at all between how she mistreated men, women, administrative assistants, other managers, even visiting vendors and folks who had the misfortune to bring lunch deliveries into that building located a few degrees southeast of hell.

No matter the age or experience, occupation or station, she took her particular neuroses out on *every*one.

Anyone who's spent time playing and suffering in the Corporate American Chain of Command Games won't be the least bit surprised to hear she got promoted constantly. VP of acquisitions and mergers somewhere last time I heard.

Mike Billings, on the other hand, seems to have made it his professional mission to target young women just starting out. Not just any woman, not that that wouldn't be bad enough.

He reserved his Grade-A nastiness for the best and brightest.

The ones destined to leave him behind, in other words, if they survived long enough.

The ones who might very well catch on to how much he *didn't* know, or even worse, point out something he'd screwed up. They might even (gasp) refuse to keep his failure secret after having to clean up his ineffectual mess.

So I faced a crowd all dressed like I was, in blue-jean business-extremely-casual, looking to me for some kind of inspiration. Or guidance. Or at least a coherent agenda.

And I had no freaking clue what to say.

I just stood there gripping my coffee tankard, staring everywhere but into anyone's eyes.

Wondering when someone would have mercy and either step in or hit me with a tranquilizer dart strong enough to neutralize the obscene amounts of calories and coffee ricocheting around my system.

Then Laura finally caught my eye. And all she did was smile.

I glanced at Tia next, sitting right there in the front row with all those strangers.

Wide-eyed and expectant.

Excited.

Confident enough for both of us.

"I won't repeat the reasons we're here," I said. "I figure since y'all came all the way up here and got up this damn early on a Saturday, you don't need me to remind you of anything. I will say thank you, and thank you even more to Millie and her fearless sidekicks for feeding us within an inch of our lives."

Everyone stood, turned toward Millie and her friends waiting around their makeshift kitchen, and clapped and cheered. Seeing our gang of chefs grin and turn bright red was all the ice-breaking my nerves needed.

"I think we've all got our parts rehearsed and ready to go," I went on when they settled down. "Of course that's not especially hard to do, whether you're years out from Mike and his bullshit or just ran across it yesterday. We're all in this together, and we're going to take care of each other, and take care of what needs to be done."

I paused long enough to let Tia soak in a bit of that much-needed solidarity. When she smiled at me, fighting back tears, I knew she was in the right place.

"Our dear communications coordinator Edgar will have the guest of honor here by eight, so we've got a bit more time for last-minute questions or arrangements or bouts of panic, whatever might seem appropriate. The truth is I believe we've got it all covered."

I waved one hand toward the row of brick grills.

"If you've somehow managed not to hear about Laura and me managing our great escape from corporate torment a couple of weeks ago, you may not know what I thought the crazy number of grills all over this mountain might be for. I wondered if they were for cutting down on the food budget while dealing with escapees like us."

I waited for the laughter to die down, especially after Millie shrugged and mimed zipping her lips.

"Now, not all of you are as...vintage as I am, so you may not remember when assholes like Mike were called male chauvinist pigs. Well, we may or may not get around to using the grills, but today our little piggy is going to get his long-overdue roasting."

7

There were only a few nervous giggles at first, and I wasn't sure whether I'd overshot with that one or not. But gradually one woman, then another, then everyone including the good guys went from giggles, to laughter, to whoops and hollers, and finally to standing up and cheering.

I had to admit standing there in a group of the smartest women and best men I knew and yelling my fool head off in the middle of the woods right along with them brought a significant and unaccustomed amount of joy to my black little heart.

We'd done everything we could to get ready.

Now it was a matter of keeping our cool and bringing the whole thing together.

Laura and Tia both headed straight for me as

soon as we all started milling around and shaking off too much nervous energy.

"That was *great*, sugar." Laura laid a kiss on me that livened me up almost as much as the coffee. "I told you you'd do just fine."

"We'll see how long that prediction holds up once we're actually underway," I said, grinning like a crazy woman. "But I sure do appreciate the thought and the smooch."

Tia pretended to look away while all that was going on, but I think she was secretly fascinated by the mating habits of her nerd-elders out in the wild.

"So I know we talked about me staying out of sight," she said, "and I'll gladly do that if you think it's best. But I think I might want to...I don't know, be part of this myself. Maybe at least sit in the back in case I want to speak up?"

My gaze met Laura's, and I knew we were both thinking the same thing.

She confirmed it with her words a second later.

"I doubt anyone here would stop you from doing whatever you want, Tia. Just keep in mind good jobs aren't as easy to come by as they were when Angie and I were your age, about a hundred years ago. You're damn good, and that's the truth. But no one wants to see you get hurt by him any more than you already have been."

Tia nodded, staring at the ground, then looked up with her chin held high, and her gorgeous black hair gleaming in the sun.

"I'll read the room, you know? Or the pavilion, anyway. Because the truth is *no* job is a good one with a jackass like Mike breathing down my neck and waiting to pounce at the smallest sign of self-confidence. If this doesn't make a difference, I'll need to get myself into a better situation no matter what. But I hope I get to stay. You'll probably get sick of my questions sooner than you think, Angie."

"Challenge accepted," I said, holding up my tankard for a tap against her miniature version. "Keep 'em coming and help keep an old lady on her toes."

Edie came rushing toward us then, her face set in a determined scowl that didn't give me an especially warm or fuzzy feeling.

Which is strange, because the sight of Edie with her spectacular waves of curly hair in every color under the sun, glorious variety of earrings, and fabulous outfit of vivid purple jeans and a black shirt decorated with rainbow rows of tiny zeros and ones would normally send me into the oddball bliss of my kind of people.

"Just got a text from Edgar," she said. "Which I would have gotten at least an hour ago if we got even a greedy scrap of cellular signal in this tech-forsaken place like everyone else back down in the twenty-first century. Mike of course wanted to get an extra-early start, and declared he'd simply drive himself if Edgar wasn't ready in time."

I did my best not to clench my teeth, but my contentedly full belly took on the contractions for itself.

"I'll bet Mike had all kinds of charming and regressive justifications for that little change of plans," I said. "How bad is it?"

"Oh yeah, from the unmissable *tone* in Edgar's text, Mike's got himself into full knight-in-shining-armor mode, and he's oh-so-very-desperate to rescue us poor damsels in distress. They'll be here in about ten minutes, and that was hoping for bad traffic. Thank the gods of paranoia and doing everything way ahead of time, I made all my special prepara-tions to the pavilion last night. But we still need to get this place looking conference-legitimate."

Laura grunted and rolled her eyes.

"Traffic isn't likely to save us once they get north of the city this time of day, even during the week. All right, time to find another gear and get this show underway."

At her much louder announcement of our greatly accelerated timeframe, the most efficient and effective low-grade panic you could possibly imagine set in. No one got angry or yelled at each other, though an impressive number of adult words found their way out into the North Georgia morning air.

Everyone jumped into motion, and my entirely ornery and inappropriate mind turned the whole scene into fast-forward on an old VCR, squeaky voices and everything.

We got all the chairs lined up, folders distributed, complimentary coffee cups set out, and ourselves seated in the correct order with a speed that would have impressed Atlanta drivers in those rare and exhilarating moments between snarled traffic and snarling drivers, when there's room to let your car stretch out and strut its stuff.

Two rows of women up front, with the great guys scattered in beside their partners to help give Mike a false sense of masculine camaraderie.

We were down to the last-minute mic checks and such by the time a suitably impressive charcoal-gray sedan rolled into view through the trees along the curving gravel road. Edie assured us Edgar was not normally anywhere near that sedate or cautious a driver, so he was making every effort to give us time to adjust for his abrupt arrival.

I'm not sure what I thought the hardest part was going to be before it circled around my mind and nerves like dirty dishwater circling the drain, but I know it wasn't having to sit there and pretend to be normal.

I mean, aside from the half-assed efforts I'd made to blend in when the situation demanded it since I was about eight years old.

Now I had to bust out my very best acting chops and sit quietly, but not too quiet. Face forward rather than staring at the newly arrived car, but not sitting rigid as a statue dedicated to the theme of high anxiety.

Appear to converse in a friendly manner with the women around me, without babbling incoherently or letting my voice drift up into some variety of manic and shrill.

Hell, the simple effort required to stop myself from bursting into bouts of uncontrolled giggles drained me within a few drops of my bloodstream's coffee levels.

Luckily for all of us, we had years of experience in doing all of that, in places like this resort, and with people we liked an awful lot less than we liked each other.

Anyone who's ever endured more than their fair share of corporate meetings has spent too much time developing this particular skill set.

We finally heard two car doors shut, followed by

Millie calling out a cheery greeting—not at all manic or worried, because she's just that damn good—offering Edgar and Mike something to eat or drink.

And I swear I didn't make this next part up, mainly because you *can't* make shit like this up.

We heard Edgar politely ask for coffee and a whole-wheat bagel, while somehow managing not to sound like he'd just spent hours in the company of one of the most unpleasant humans to ever make it to middle age.

All my barely held restraint and desire to make sure the plans came to fruition wouldn't have stopped me from screaming, possibly wailing, and quite likely pulling clumps of my hair out.

But for Mike, polite or even neutral flat-out never seemed to cross his mind when it came to interacting with a woman. Especially one Millie's age, or in front of a guy he probably assumed shared his low opinion of the *fairer* sex.

The words that slimed their way out of his mouth were, "Just run and fetch me the cup, hon, and I'll take care of the rest myself. I'd hate to start my day off with the kind of pink sugary concoction you girls consider coffee."

8

The chorus of sighs around me sounded like the trees reluctantly parting with their last few colorful autumn leaves, as if they'd finally been forced to admit they weren't going to amount to much after all. No matter how hard they'd worked over the summer to raise them right and send them out into the world to make their own way.

Sometimes even a tree has to learn to cut her losses and move on.

Edie got up then and squeezed my shoulder on her way past.

Hard enough to leave a bruise, I'm sure. And I don't blame her.

Taking on her assigned role as conference coordinator, and hopefully not slugging Mike a good one right across the mouth.

No matter how much he'd earned it.

"Good morning, Mr. Billings," she said, smooth and sweet as whipped honey. "We're *so* glad you could make it. We're just about ready to get started if you want to get yourself settled and seated."

Mike let out what could only be described as an *oily* chuckle.

"Well, I didn't expect you'd be able to get this show on the road without the guest of honor. Someone equipped to take on a much-needed leadership role. Otherwise these young gals could get themselves off on the wrong foot and into all kinds of trouble. Easier and better to nip that kind of thing in the bud, don't you think?"

I hadn't realized until that exact moment that I despised the word "gals" even more than "girls" in that tone of voice, or being called young lady when I was a kid.

Especially when Mike said it.

But Edie only laughed, and it sounded light and natural as could be.

I myself was glaring so hard at one of the cracks in the mortar around the fireplace bricks that it's a pure wonder the whole structure didn't collapse and put an early and merciful end to us all.

"That *is* why we invited you, Mr. Billings," she

said. "We couldn't be happier to present everyone with such a once-in-a-lifetime opportunity today."

I hadn't realized how hard my leg was jumping until Laura put her hand on my knee. She leaned toward me and whispered.

"Maintain. He's making this a lot easier on everyone."

"Easy enough to go to Plan B, as in barbecue him and bury the bones up here after the feast?"

Laura shook her head, even though her eyes sparkled.

"Tempting as that might be, I'm not sure we're ready to force Millie and her friends to work the grill at Camp Cannibal."

I barely fought back a snort and did my best to glare at Laura, who had the gall to wink and make it even worse.

The only thing that could have put a stop to the epic laughing fit brewing itself in my belly was the sight of Mike and his Superior Smarmy Smile.

He walked around the front of the group, one of Millie's delectable poppyseed bagels clutched in one hand, a brilliant pink and entirely reusable coffee cup in the other. I kid you not, he somehow managed to hold the cup and sneer down at it without missing a step.

Edie walked a half-step behind him, cheerful and

bright as the eyelashes on Millie's sunshine-on-wheels truck. If no one has thought of hiring Edie for any of the movie and television productions constantly filming in Atlanta and all over Georgia, they're missing a Golden Globe opportunity.

We'd set up seven chairs up front, facing the crowd, with their folders neatly placed on the seats, but no one sat there yet. Every eye on that mountain saw Mike glance that way, certain he was meant to be the center of attention from the start.

After all, besides Edgar—who'd surely removed himself to the back row to inhale his coffee and bagel in peace, but still with a good view—and the brave men who'd made the trip in support, Mike absolutely saw himself as the only *man* in a huge group of *gals*.

I'm amazed his overinflated ego didn't bust out and tear him into a million slimy arrogant shreds of less-than-mediocre middle-manager right then and there.

But he was far too gallant to leave the rest of us delicate flowers helpless and alone in a frightening IT world our teeny female brains couldn't possibly comprehend.

Edie waved him toward the chairs up front, waiting long enough for him to head toward the one in the middle before she touched his shoulder. When she pointed toward the one on the end, furthest from the lectern, Mike turned to her with his eyebrows raised, obviously certain she'd made a mistake with her addleheaded feminine brain.

With a smile I never could have managed without a good kick to his gut, Edie nodded and again pointed toward the end.

Mike didn't bother trying to hide his head shake and eyeroll, but he did take his seat.

Exactly where we wanted him.

And when Edie walked down the middle of the group of women—winking at me—our girl-nerd party got itself started.

First order of business?

Waiting.

While Mike made a show of settling himself, sipping his coffee from the offending non-disposable cup, and arranging the unopened folder with those subtly threatening rows of near-faceless women on his lap, we all sat quietly.

Staring at him.

Not scowling or frowning, or even laughing, though I'm quite sure I wasn't the only one who had a hell of a time keeping a neutral expression.

Simply watching him, with no emotion at all.

Much like the cartoon women gazing out from the folders and notebooks.

No sounds besides the morning breeze and birds chattering about the warm sunshine.

Even Millie and her catering crew stood in a line to the side and stared at Mike while he finished chomping down his bagel.

Just like Laura predicted when she came up with this delightfully evil opening move, it took an embarrassingly long time for him to catch on.

He'd made the whole thing one hell of a lot easier by insisting on showing up so damn early and throwing us into a rush to get ready.

After enough minutes passed that I gritted my teeth to keep from jumping up and screaming at him to notice the world around him for a change, even if that world was populated only with women, he finally looked up.

Just a quick glance at first as he wiped his mouth and crumpled up his napkin, but then his head popped up like a prairie dog checking for predators. Mike's eyes darted back and forth for a few seconds before he slowly turned his head from one side to the other. Probably searching for a sympathetic male gaze and finding none.

A quick clearing of his throat led to shifting in his seat led to brushing at his flyaway hair.

I could *feel* him straining to avoid looking at his watch.

When he finally did, a second sigh passed through his rapt audience, this one a good bit rougher-edged. More like the first grim wind gust of a cold front moving in.

With that agreed-upon trigger, Edie walked back up the middle aisle, purple jeans and rainbow hair and glorious computer-code shirt catching every shred of sunlight. Holding her own steaming ceramic tureen full of caffeinated joy graced with our fabulous staring-women avatars.

She swept up onto the stage and graced us with a diabolical smile.

"It's *truly* my pleasure to welcome all of you to the Securing the Ladder conference. I certainly hope you'll be glad you decided to give up a day of your precious weekend by the time we finish. The topic for this morning is near and dear to my heart, as I'm sure it is to many of yours. Let's jump right in with Managing Misogyny in the Workplace."

9

Mike's eyebrows shot up again, this time followed by a confused scowl. He flipped the folder on his lap open.

I didn't have to open mine to know he'd be reading that same title at the top of one of Millie's gorgeous glossy pages. Instead of speaking up, reading the faux description, or even raising his hand to ask what was going on, he only closed the folder and stared at Millie.

Still looking confused, to be sure, and making a sadly ineffective attempt to hide it.

Not a trace of recognition, though, or any kind of awareness that the topic might turn out to be a bit uncomfortable for him.

My money was on Mike not catching a clue the topic was even *relevant* to him.

Not yet.

"Rather than following the same standard-issue corporate sensitivity training blueprint we've all suffered through too many times," Edie said, pausing for a scattering of applause, "we decided to approach the topic through the more compassionate lens of true, lived experience. Once we've had time to hear how things honestly have been out there, and how they still are now, we'll discuss ways to make the changes that are so sadly overdue."

Mike finally squirmed in his seat, undoubtedly again searching for a Y-chromosome-equipped person to smirk with through such estrogen-charged madness.

I'd spent enough time talking with the men in attendance—and watching their faces while we women discussed our plans—to know he wasn't getting a damn thing besides stony stares.

"So we'll start at the beginning." Edie stepped to the side and held out one hand. "With an example of how this kind of gender discrimination can start even before day one on the job."

She retook her seat beside me without so much as a glance my way, or any other sign that she was up to anything except handling introductions.

One of the women who'd had the misfortune to collide with Mike during her hiring interview walked up front, stunning and luscious in an indigo blouse that set off her waves of thick black-streaked-with-silver hair flowing nearly to her faded jeans. When she turned, my mind served up a vision of her in a brilliant sari, maybe on her wedding day, with intricate henna designs on her hands and sparkling jewels around her neck.

But what stood out most was the fierce intelligence that flashed from her green eyes.

If I'd been Mike facing her down when she was furious, I believe I would have fainted to the floor in a puddle, even decades ago.

"Thank you, Edie, and thank you everyone for inviting me," she said, with only a trace of a lilt in her mostly unaccented Atlanta voice. "I'm Pasha, and I've been working in IT for more than thirty years. I'm currently managing a team of young engineers and programmers working on HVAC systems for building complexes."

I'm quite sure I wasn't the only one more than a little impressed, since we hadn't talked about our current gigs while planning this mountaintop shindig. But of course, Mike only crossed his arms and frowned.

"One of the most important lessons for me came early on," Pasha continued. "During my first round of interviews, so you might say before I truly got a start. And that lesson, unpleasant though it was, shaped my entire career. One of the interviewers seemed determined to disqualify me before I could get even a toe in the door. This person came after me with dozens of questions I wouldn't need to answer for years, turning my lack of experience into an accusation of complete ignorance. And when that wasn't enough to dissuade me, they accused me of lying on my résumé."

Pasha never glanced Mike's way, or gestured toward him, or slipped up one time in her refusal to even say a *man* did these things. And yet, a pink flush started at Mike's collar and rose toward his chin.

"Despite that harsh introduction to the job, and the interviewer's efforts to drive me away, other recruiters gave me a fair chance. I got the job, and I kept it for a time. It wouldn't have been a bad place to get my start, except the same interviewer continued to undermine me and belittle me. As if I'd somehow personally offended them simply by knowing how to do the job I'd earned, and making every effort to learn more. In other words, exactly what any of us *should* do in that situation."

She shook her head, and her lovely features twisted in disgust.

"In case you're wondering, young *men* did not suffer the same treatment. I left as soon as I found another position. Which not only means I had to go through the stress of searching and interviewing sooner than I was ready, but that the company lost a promising employee. I'm quite certain they continued to lose more young women as long as they kept that interviewer on-staff. They needed to do better. And we must do all we can to make certain such harassment doesn't follow us any further into this new millennium. Thank you."

She turned and sat in the chair furthest from Mike, smiling at the vigorous round of applause from everyone besides him.

Mike only stared straight ahead, the frown never leaving his face.

Three more women spoke, each recounting their Mike-based horror stories. I'd heard all of them over our first dinner at Juan's, but their words in front of this group of women stirred up a combination of anger and sympathy intense enough to make my head pound.

Taking me back to my own experience with him was part of it, sure. Most was knowing I hadn't been singled out.

For once, the proof that a nightmare situation hadn't been the least bit personal didn't make me feel better.

Because he'd been free to do the same to other

women, and cunning enough to move on before anyone could put a stop to it, or even warn the next woman headed toward his chauvinist grinding wheel.

The worst—at least for me—was Ansi, a tall, athletic-looking woman with her silver hair buzzed close, who recounted a story all too close to mine. She'd been setting up laptops for people in her law firm to take on trips, way back in the Dark Ages when most of us didn't have at least a couple sitting around at home, so companies kept a supply of expensive loaners.

She'd quite appropriately noticed not only illegal, non-licensed software on the installation file copied onto the laptops (a potentially serious problem for a law firm, of all things), but a confidential HR spreadsheet with every single employee's pay and benefits hitching a ride in the Documents folder, all the way up to the partners (a *massive* problem for *any* kind of firm).

But after Ansi pointed it out to her manager, not even realizing Mike had created that installation file, Mike busted his ass to turn her life into a living hell at that firm. Including convincing more than enough people that *she'd* made the mistake instead of him.

Ansi'd handled everything far better than I had with my work-bridge-demolition spree, by carefully documenting every instance of Mike's mistakes and his abuse, therefore earning herself a fantastic severance package on her way out the door in exchange for keeping quiet.

But the experience had soured her on the field, sending her instead into a wildly successful career change as the badass attorney who'd done quite well cleaning up this kind of bullshit herself in workplace and government alike.

Not a bad person to have on our side for sure.

Especially since she left most of that spectacular post-IT career news out while she spoke a few feet away from Mike. As far as he knew, she'd only found a new line of work.

Surely too ordinary to mention.

Still, the look in her eyes while she was talking made it clear the humiliation and anger that drove her onto such a different path again bubbled uncomfortably close to the surface.

And that left me seething at how an insecure, unskilled parasite of a nasty human being had gotten away with this kind of behavior for so fucking long.

10

Turned out I wasn't the only one building up to the boiling point, even though not one woman had used Mike's name or so much as glanced his way.

And turned out he had a better memory for his run-ins with these troublesome *gals* than he did for any technical skills that might have actually let him advance in his career like so many of us had.

By the time Mike sat up front with several women and only one empty seat between himself and them, and when my buddy Rosita stood to take her turn, he cleared his throat rude and loud enough to be overheard all the way back in Atlanta.

Rosita started toward the front anyway.

So Mike set his empty coffee cup and folder down, making a petulant racket with each one.

Stepping up onto the stage, Rosita turned toward us with a luminous—and expectant—smile.

Mike held up his hand like a little boy in school, but only for a second.

His face screwed into that little boy's first-rate-temper-tantrum scowl, and he jumped to his feet.

"Please excuse my interruption, *ladies*. But I'm starting to wonder what I'm doing here at your little pity party that you call a conference. Anyone care to enlighten me?"

Rosita hesitated long enough to take a slow breath, as if she was breathing in the sweet perfume of the first flowers of spring after a brutally long winter. Then she turned to Mike, still smiling.

"If you care to look at your schedule, Mr. Billings," she soothed, "I'm sure you'll see we're following the presentation for this morning as planned."

All traces of his suit of protective smugness armor vanished, he jammed his hands onto his hips.

"You honestly *planned* to listen to a bunch of sob stories? And pretend to *learn* something from it? About the only thing anyone would learn from this is how to toughen up and get over it. Or heaven forbid I say *man* up, even though that's clear as day what needs to happen!"

Rosita folded her hands and held her head to one

side. I'd known her long enough to see the pursed lips, one eyebrow raised, what-the-*hell*-is-wrong-with-you look as if she'd turned it on me.

Again.

Her smooth as honey and twice as sweet voice was another warning sign.

"Mr. Billings, in case you're having difficulty understanding, the point is no one should suffer abuse like this. Not at work or anywhere else. And no one should feel justified in behaving this way. *Manning up*, as you so unoriginally put it, isn't the point when it comes to supporting young people entering our field. Not for the confident, experienced, mature adults who have the most to share. Mentoring them, teaching them, bringing them along to be the next generation of successful professionals is the goal."

Mike glared out at us, narrowed eyes darting from one man to another. Obviously looking for backup and not finding it.

"And all of you so-called *men* are okay with this? Sitting there and watching a bunch of moaning little girls tell you how bad you are at your jobs? And why they should push you out of the way and take over? So they can set up weekly sharing circles and sympathy groups and period parties, or whatever feminist nonsense they insist on next?"

I heard someone move their chair back and stand behind me.

"Sounds to me like you should sit down and keep your mouth shut," a deep voice said. "Since you have even less of a grasp on what's going on here than anyone expected."

More movement, and another man spoke.

"Might want to ask yourself what you're so afraid of. Or maybe why women wanting to be treated like equals bothers you."

Mike flung both arms out.

"The fact that I didn't have time then and don't have time now to teach remedial information technology to a bunch of girls doesn't mean I'm afraid. It's not my job to drag herds of unqualified females along until they finally manage to make up for their own deficiencies. If you want to take that on, be my guest. Just leave me out of it."

Instead of feeling panic-stricken or finding myself in the extremely unusual situation of not knowing what to say when this moment came, I had to restrain myself from leaping onto the stage and putting myself within smacking distance.

"See, that's the thing, isn't it, Mike?" I managed to keep my voice down, but the words came out bitten-off and razor sharp. "These weren't unqualified or inept or remedial people then, and they're not now. Did you miss the part where everyone who spoke is a project manager or a head engineer or a senior developer? Or successful as hell in another line of work? These are people who were ambitious and smart and determined when they started out. And once they got a chance to prove it, they *turned* out to be all that and more."

Laura stood beside me, and I'd swear on a stack of brand-new tech manuals that the disgust rolled off her in waves.

"Maybe that's the part that bugs you, huh?" she said. "How despite your best efforts to push these women back and run them down and drive them away, they kept on fighting. They kept on learning and succeeding and getting better at what they do. Moving ahead instead of getting caught in the same job, the same ridiculous bullying routine. The same pathetic story that was already old and stale when *Reagan* was in office."

Mike's face took on a poisonous grin and he crossed his arms.

"So now you're admitting I *helped* your careers, huh? That if you delicate flowers hadn't crossed paths with me, you might have been coddled and sheltered and padded into keeping the same jobs for decades? Yeah, I recognize a bunch of you now. Sounds to me like everyone here should be *thanking* me instead of putting on this silly weep-fest."

Ansi didn't stand or raise her voice, and she didn't need to. Her simple head-turn toward Mike and hint of a smile captured all of our attention.

Except the one person who should have been paying at least half the attention to her that she'd been paying to him.

"So you're saying you not only recognize these stories, but that you are in fact the person each woman described?"

Mike laughed, and the somehow *oily* sound of it made my skin crawl.

"What kind of idiot do you take me for? Of course it was me, and you know that as well as I do, girlie. *You're* the one who couldn't wait to scurry up to management with what you'd found and try to get *my* head on the chopping block. How'd that work out for you? Oh wait, you just admitted it in front of everyone. You connived a way to get them to pay you off to get your whining out of everyone's hair and keep your mouth shut, but *I* didn't go anywhere until *I* decided to."

Even the breeze and the birds joined us in holding our breath.

Waiting to see how Ansi would nudge him to twist and weave the trap.

"So you might say you purposely targeted these women?"

Mike snorted, an ugly, harsh sound, and gestured toward Ansi and the other women on the stage.

"Just look around. You heard what they said, and I doubt anyone else lined up to come up here and sing her pitiful song will do any better. Not a single one of you was cut out to handle the work, to the surprise of no one besides yourselves. How much hand-holding are we men supposed to do until you finally catch up? If you ever do."

Ansi didn't bat an eye or change the tone of her voice.

"So you might say you purposely targeted these women?"

Mike rounded on her then, leaning forward with his fists clenched.

"Of course I did! The managers I worked with were just as gutless and weak as the token *men* you dragged up here for this farce of a conference. You think I was going to stand back and let you *ladies* take over and destroy my workplace, then bust my ass cleaning up your perfume-stinking mess? Just let you turn our lives into a living hell? Or take things into my own hands and get the job done!"

11

Ansi never flinched.

But she did smile.

Showing her neat, even teeth that time.

"I must say I find it fascinating that you don't hesitate to admit harassment, Mr. Billings, and in front of the women you harassed."

"Harassment? Oh come on, *Ansi*. Like I just said, I did you all a favor. Sounds like a bunch of you found places to work where you could manage to learn the job, eventually, without someone being oh-so-mean to you because you failed at everything you *pretended* to know on your résumé. With a crew of hand-holders on staff willing to get you up to speed. But I'd say my best work was getting the weakest ones like you to move the hell on and find work better suited to your delicate temperaments. What are you, huh? A kitten snuggler? Maybe a flower whisperer at the botanical gardens?"

Ansi rose with fluid grace, standing several inches taller than Mike.

"While I do quite enjoy kittens, and flowers, and especially puppies, Mr. Billings, I did manage to find my way to a profession equally suited to my talents and personality. I changed sides, you see. Instead of supporting attorneys, I became one myself. Specializing in labor relations and harassment in the workplace. Yes, including gender bias and intimidation."

Mike took a deep breath and opened his mouth, no doubt ready to spew forth what he thought was an exceedingly clever and biting retort.

Then we saw Ansi's words slowly making their way through his weak and bitter gray matter and finally hitting their target.

Have you ever seen a person deflate?

I had too, but not like this. Mike could have been a model for a cartoonist that day. He shrank and wilted so much I was surprised his clothes didn't fall right off him.

But of all the things I'm thankful for, the fact that he didn't end up standing there nekkid has to be at the top of the list.

His voice drifted through the air like smoke.

"You're a lawyer? You specialize in..."

His gaze finally tore itself away from Ansi, who calmly watched with her dangerous smile. He turned and slowly took in the rest of us, almost like he'd forgotten any of us were there. Eyes wide, mouth open but not spewing bullshit for a damn change.

I don't know about anyone else, but I had a harder time than I expected keeping myself from laughing. The only thing that saved me was being too afraid I'd interrupt whatever was kludging its way through his mind.

This was one scenario I most definitely wanted to see play itself out to the end.

"So this whole thing was a trap," Mike said in a stronger voice. "Lure the poor old sexist dinosaur out to the woods and make a fool of him, or try to." He shook his head like he was about to scold one of Ansi's puppies for a house-training accident. "Talk about pathetic. All this time and fussing and expense so you can get your giggles and go back to your dainty little sheltered lives? Sure hope it was worth it."

Without any kind of planning or cue besides a bone-deep, intense awareness that the time was right, almost everyone but Mike sat.

Leaving Edie facing him from the other side of the stage.

"I'd say it was well worth it, Mr. Billings. You

don't know it yet, but things are going to be different from here on out."

Mike's laugh was a touch more manic than nervous, but not by much.

"You think so, do you? Got a bunch more of my supposed victims hidden away somewhere to parade their poor-pitiful-me stories to wrap up this hen fest? Sorry to tell you I'm not impressed, or interested. I won't be partaking of any more of your manufactured drama."

Edie laughed throaty and low—the sort of laugh that could disarm the most curmudgeonly old snot of any gender in ten seconds flat.

Except this version carried a scalpel-sharp edge deep down inside where it'd be easy to miss.

"Oh Mike, I'm afraid you don't understand. Whether you're interested in partaking or not couldn't possibly be more irrelevant." She pointed at one of the thick wooden beams that made up the roof of our cozy pavilion's shelter. "Take a look. See the shiny bits, just there? They resemble eyes, really, maybe of some kind of insect. Dare I say a praying mantis would fit the bill in this case?"

Mike glared at her for several of his own hitching breaths, his face getting more twisted and red by the second. I couldn't help glancing at his feet, waiting for the pissed off little-kid stomp I was convinced we'd get treated to next.

He finally cut his gaze toward the beam for a quick second.

All the color and tension distorting his face fled in an instant.

But his voice came back as spiteful and loud as ever.

"Assuming those things are real and you have any clue how to set them up, how nice for you to have the spare time and money to waste on recordings. I'm sure you'll enjoy re-watching them around your knit-and-bitch wine circles and weep-fest movie nights. Because I don't care how many skirt-lawyers you have brainwashed or blackmailed into this estrogen-fueled revenge fantasy of yours. If you try to do anything else with the tapes, I'll send in a swarm of *real* attorneys and take every last one of you down."

Edie shook her head with a sad smile.

"Didn't anyone ever teach you about reading everything you sign, Mr. Billings? Especially when it comes to image and video release clauses? Or are you the sort who clicks right through terms and conditions windows without a glance when you're installing software, too?"

My urge to stand up and yell something quite unladylike about how Mike sometimes didn't bother with *legal* software, so of course he didn't give a damn about terms and conditions was fierce enough that Laura put a firm hand on my knee to stop me.

I suppose that was Ansi's thunder if she wanted to use it.

And she only watched Mike with that devastating smile.

She'd probably faced down more assholes in court than I'd encountered in IT, which was a particularly horrifying reality.

For Mike's part, now he seemed frozen, like a clockwork version of a human that had abruptly wound down. When he finally managed to shake his head, the herky-jerky movement reminded me of one of those toys with sand in its gears.

His voice had that same grinding quality.

"I didn't sign anything like that."

12

I knew without a backward glance that the person now strolling toward the front was Edgar, taking his revenge for putting up with Mike's pompous ass for weeks, and especially on what must have been the longest drive in the history of Atlanta traffic.

I hadn't seen Edgar for a few days, so I raised my hand to cover my grin. Rather than his usual fabulous short spiky hair, as brilliantly colored as Edie's, he sported a perfect corporate-bland side part in a most flattering shade of brunette. His equally appealing charcoal-gray slacks and golf shirt—a perfect match for the sedan he'd rented to squire Mike to our evil soiree—might have come from a high-end Midtown shop called Dress to Depress Any Workplace Interest in Your Personal Life.

I was willing to bet all the delectable break-time

goodies Millie had waiting for us that Edgar was absolutely itching to get back to his preferred multi-hued wardrobe.

But his smile made it clear the reward was easily worth the discomfort at the moment.

"*So* sorry to contradict you, Mr. Billings," Edgar said in his best soothing overnight radio DJ voice. "One of my responsibilities as part of helping orga-nize our Securing the Ladder conference is keeping track of every participant's information and signed release forms. I've got yours right here if you'd like to take a look."

He whipped a tastefully expensive black leather folder out from under his arm and offered it with the same flair as a waiter presenting a bottle of the week's most trendy and exclusive booze for a demanding client's inspection.

"But I can assure you everything is in order," Edgar went on. "Including the image and video release portion of the contract, and your signature agreeing to the whole thing."

Ansi leaned toward Mike. "And *I* can assure you the entire contract is properly written and executed, Mr. Billings. This hen fest, as you so charmingly called it, wanted to be certain their contract was iron-clad. So I insisted on writing it myself."

Mike shook his head very slowly, the movement gradually picking up speed with his words.

"What the hell are you trying to do, then? Blackmail me? Upload this garbage to the internet? Use it as a recruiting tool for your feminist training camps? What was the *point*?"

"I think you might have enjoyed this part, Mike," Laura said, in what I'd come to recognize as her sugar-cookie-loaded-with-arsenic voice. "Too bad you weren't there. See, we discussed several different ideas over a lovely dinner. If we'd had sewing with us, you probably would have called it a stitch-and-bitch circle. Anyway, there were some *great* ideas. A job interview scenario, where we made you demonstrate your skill level against ours. A mock trial, with a judge and witnesses and a jury and all. Possibly a game show format, laugh track included, maybe with a bucket of slime overhead for the loser."

She rubbed her hands together and let out a positively gleeful laugh that raised goosebumps along my arms.

"There were other ideas, of course, once we got around to dessert and cocktails. I still say it's a damn shame most of them are illegal in Georgia and under federal law, and definitely a violation of the Geneva Convention."

Mike somehow managed to not only turn pale,

but put on an expression that reminded me of cheap, way-past-its-prime cottage cheese.

"But we eventually decided that the *point* was to speak and be heard. To have the chance to tell the truth without a bunch of gaslighting bullshit, for the first time for some of us. We knew there was pretty much zero chance you'd listen or acknowledge a word any of us said. You've proven us right like a champ there. So we're here to do that for each other. Having you as a witness is the sweet bonus that makes the whole thing worthwhile."

Mike snarled without adjusting his spoiled-cottage-cheese consistency.

"Well, bully for you. What exactly do you expect me to do about it?"

My turn had rolled around again, and I wasn't the slighted bit nervous now, or even angry. Not really.

I was more...locked in and ready.

"That depends on you, Mike," I said. "Are you planning to keep up your abusive bullshit? Keep believing women in IT have cooties or are out to steal your job or whatever's kept you acting this way for almost *forty* years? Or are you going to drag yourself kicking and screaming into the twenty-first century? If you do that, we're all good. Nothing for you to worry about."

Laura spoke up beside me again.

"But if you keep on with your caveman ways, this video will find its way to wherever it needs to go. HR departments, hiring managers, labor law attorneys. It's the information age, right? So people should know who they're dealing with."

A puzzled frown crossed Ansi's face.

"One might call it miraculous that you haven't been brought up on harassment charges before. I suspect the days of you skating by with a bunch of other desperate defenders of the mothballed Good Old Boy network have come to a long-overdue end."

Renee—the Black woman with delightfully spiky braids who was quite possibly the intellectual champ of our group—stood.

"And don't bother trying to convince yourself we won't know how your personal escape from misogyny project is coming along, Mike. See, I believe you know deep down inside just how damn good we all are at what we do. I suspect that's one of the main reasons you targeted us and who knows how many other brilliant young women along the way. What I can *promise* is we already know a lot more than we're letting on today. That won't change in the foreseeable future."

She raised one hand and pointed at him to emphasize her words.

"It's *way* past time for you...to do...better."

Mike's foul dairy product demeanor shifted between one breath and the next. He stood up tall and held up both hands, his usual smarmy smirk back in place.

"Okay, okay, ladies, you got me. I haven't exactly been the most modern of coworkers, I understand that. Can't say that I blame you for calling me out on how I've behaved in the past. Or I guess I should say *mis*behaved."

If I'd had the slightest whisper of a doubt about him somehow attaining even deeper levels of horse-shit, that last line would have cured me right quick.

So of course he kept talking to make sure no one missed his epic levels of fecal stockpiling accomplishment.

"What you're missing is how I've already gotten so much better. It's been hard work, but I know it's worth it. Why, Angie and Laura can back me up on this, because I made a point of taking a job with an all-female help desk where they work! Would I have done that if I hadn't changed?"

I felt Laura lean forward at the same time I did—no doubt every bit as willing and eager to finally put Mike out of our misery—but a quiet voice from behind me stopped us both cold.

"I'll back you up on it."

13

I turned to see Tia, face red but determined. Young as I'd thought she looked moping in the break room, now she looked like a middle-schooler to my grizzled old eyes.

The sure sign of her being into her twenties and furious showed in the high fire in *her* eyes.

She tucked her waterfall of glossy black hair behind her ears and raised her chin.

"I can absolutely verify that Mr. Billings recently took a job managing the help desk where Angie and Laura work. Because I work there too. I'm sure you remember me, Mr. Billings. From the data breach yesterday? I know it's fresh in *my* mind."

Mike tried to back up a step and almost tripped over his chair.

"I'm not sure this is the time for a discussion of help desk reporting protocol."

"I say it's the perfect time." Tia smiled, and it showed signs of someday blossoming into the same expert-level-dangerous as Ansi's. "We are indeed an all-woman team, and the mentorship and learning opportunities and training have been first-rate. Best in the city as far as I'm concerned. Or it was, until a new help desk manager came onboard."

Now Mike held up both hands, and no one could miss his agitated, wide-eyed glance at Edie's cameras.

"And you're one of the best recruits on the team, Tia. I've said so since day one. Dedicated and a quick learner, no one would say otherwise."

Tia shrugged, and kept smiling.

"I haven't heard anyone say otherwise, that's true. I do bust my ass, after all. When I'm at work, you won't find anyone who works harder. That's why it's so damn frustrating to have someone *else* jump in and take the credit when I do my job particularly well. Say when I catch a network issue that's a rather nasty piece of work before anyone else does."

Tia caught my gaze and winked.

"And on top of that, I caught it just before the best network security engineer I've ever worked with headed out the door for the weekend. We're damn lucky Angie was still there, and willing to change her plans to save the company's ass. Wouldn't you say so, Mr. Billings? I mean, imagine the disaster if she hadn't been there to contain the damage. If no one on duty that night was good enough to catch the threat in time to let her know."

Now Mike nodded, and he stepped sideways this time, nearly slipping over the glossy folder he'd thumped onto the floor to proclaim his asinine hissy fit.

"Absolutely, Tia, you're completely right about that. I know how late Miss... I mean how late *Angie* had to stay to get the network back on an even keel. Perhaps this week we can have you set up a teaching session about the whole thing."

I had to force myself not to roll my eyes, and I'd put up a stack of magical unlimited storage, fail-proof backup drives that would stretch from Georgia to California that every woman was doing the same.

The inept middle-manager's eternal reward for someone who does their job better than anyone else.

More work on top of everything else they were already juggling while riding a unicycle through a minefield of Atlanta's metal road plates during a rush-hour ice storm.

Blindfolded.

Tia held one hand to her chest, obviously already aware of that backhanded little bonus.

"That *does* sound interesting, Mr. Billings. Now, should that be all about how I discovered the breach and reported it? Or how you jumped in and took credit for my work? Or maybe we can do an interpretive dance reenactment of the truly masterful way you took it upon yourself to belittle me first, and make it quite clear there was no way in hell someone so inexperienced and unskilled could have possibly understood what she was seeing? Much less know exactly what to do about it?"

Ansi shook her head, and it turned out her disappointed frown was far more heart-stopping than her smile.

"All in your past, Mr. Billings? Sounds like that's not exactly true, is it?"

"No, wait," Mike said, "just give me a chance to explain. That's not what happened yesterday at all."

We all turned back before Tia spoke, as if we were watching the best game of tennis ever played.

"Fair enough, you certainly deserve a chance to explain. Are you saying I lied, Mr. Billings? That I didn't catch that breach at all? Maybe that you didn't take credit for it? Or something else I'm not skilled or testosterone-laden enough to understand?"

"I wouldn't go so far as saying you *lied*." Mike scrubbed his hands together, now looking like a little kid who'd accidentally gotten into something sticky. "Maybe you didn't understand who to report to, how to report it. That kind of problem can get worse if procedures aren't followed. If you take too much time or tell the wrong person—"

"I'm going to have to say that's enough, Mike," I said, surprising myself, which is damn hard to do when you get to my age. "We've all heard your song and dance, and I'm not going to stand here and let you tune up on another young woman. Almost everyone here knows your games better than Tia does, though I'm delighted to say she's the one I've seen call you on your bullshit the quickest. And the best."

I smiled at Tia.

"Not sure if that means these young kids are quicker or tougher than we were, or that you're losing your sadistic touch after all these years. Either way, we did what we set out to do. You know where we stand, and what we're prepared to make happen. What happens next is entirely up to you."

Mike dropped his hands and shoved them into his pockets, then stared at Edie.

She only pointed back at the tiny cameras.

Mike closed his eyes for a second, then slumped back into his seat. Head in his hands.

He sat still long enough that the rest of us sat too, watching him.

Sick to death as I was of him and people like him, I wanted more than anything for him to give up, get up, and go away. As much fun as making good on our plans might be, the idea of the rest of us having to keep track of his regressive ass for years made me feel...

Tired.

So sick and tired of the same old nonsense that never seemed to end.

Even someone who'd developed skin as tough as mine needed a break.

But the chance to keep a great kid like Tia from having to grow such unwieldy armor in the first place gave me the incentive to keep at it.

That doesn't mean I wasn't relieved when Mike finally looked up, red-eyed and blinking.

"Okay. You've made your point. Had your fun. Gotten your revenge. Whatever you want to call it. I'm too old to go into another line of work. So, you win. I don't know exactly what that means yet, but I know when to face facts. You win."

He stared up at the ceiling with only a quick glance at the cameras, still recording away.

Then turned his gaze to Edgar.

"Are you supposed to take me back to the city? Or am I on my own for that?"

Edgar slipped the leather folder back under his arm and nodded once.

"I'd be happy to drive you, Mr. Billings. As long as we're agreed on one thing. I won't tolerate more of the endless stream of sexist bullshit chatter you tried to drown me in this morning. Not only are many of these women my friends, but I'd had more than my fill of that attitude sometime around 1987. One *whisper* of starting that up again, and you'll be hitching your way south on I-75 in my rearview mirror. Got it?"

Mike only nodded.

"Got it. Ready to go when you are."

Mike stood and walked slowly down the steps and off the stage, continuing on to Edgar's sedan without a glance back.

Edie reached for Edgar's hand.

"You sure you're going to be okay with him? Looks like he's going to be a mopey jerk all the way back to Atlanta."

Edgar raised Edie's hand for a quick kiss, then grinned.

"I expect mopey will be a huge improvement. Especially if it's the silent sort of moping. Well done today, everyone. It was my *pleasure* to play my own little sadistic part."

He followed Mike with a far sprightlier step, pausing halfway to blow all of us a kiss.

Laura's warm fingers slipped through mine.

"Think any of this worked? Or will he be back to business-as-usual Monday morning?"

After Edgar's inspiration, I couldn't resist holding her soft hand to my lips.

"Well, for one thing, I'd say we need to consider running our Securing the Ladder conference for real. That's a major win for women in tech, newbie, vintage, and everyone in between. And look over your shoulder. No matter what Mike decides to do or not to do, I know we made a difference for one person. That makes it all worthwhile for me."

Tia was busy shaking hands, getting pats on the back, and returning smiles from everyone else in attendance. Her face and eyes held a lightness and glow I hadn't seen before.

And yeah, that did make every bit of planning and effort and stress we'd all gone through worth it.

Laura watched Edgar's sedan slowly roll away before she turned back to me.

"I do believe you're right, beautiful. This turned out a thousand times better than even my most devious and elaborate imaginings. And the truth is as long as we've got Millie and her friends to stuff us all silly, everything pretty much has to turn out right in the end."

None of us had any idea how quick the change would be until we got to work Monday morning.

14

After a more celebratory Saturday night and all-day-Sunday than I care to elaborate on, Laura and I staggered into the break room together. Somehow at my usual earlier-than-necessary time, probably due to some obscure need to prove I could still survive such excess relatively unscathed.

What that meant in my fifties, of course, was that I'd be ingesting even more than my usual obscene amounts of coffee to have a chance of making it through an ordinary day in the IT trenches.

Even a small disaster might brick my battered, lovestruck brain like a rotten operating system update over a holiday weekend.

Before I could manage to pay proper attention to the golden early morning sunlight reflecting off the tastefully corporate white tables, I raised my head and sniffed.

The lights were still off, and I didn't hear anything besides the building's air handlers winding up their artificial desiccating breeze for the day. Exactly like all my other early morning quests for a bit of solitude before the zero-and-one-based storm.

Except that smell.

Laura grabbed my hand and squeezed, and her entirely irresistible giggle broke the pre-workday background noise silence.

"Don't tell me you're done in enough that the smell of coffee alone perked you up."

I took a cautious step forward, still holding her hand but moving a little in front of her.

"Not the usual office swill, no. But even the faintest waft of a properly brewed pot of ambrosia has been known to motivate my brain cells into functioning." I dropped my voice to a whisper. "But no one besides *Mike* is ever here this early, and he sure as shit doesn't know how to do anything useful. Much less conjure a drinkable cup of coffee. And that smells like *my* coffee."

Laura started to grumble something about me stepping in front of her like some kind of lesbian knight in tastefully coordinated and entirely comfortable armor, but she jumped as hard as I did when someone spoke.

"That's because you're the one who taught me how to make it."

I peeked around the corner and jumped again when Laura flipped the lights on.

I'm not proud of it, but I did let out an undignified squeak.

"Tia? What the hell are you doing here so early?"

And there she was, gorgeous hair pulled back in a ponytail that made her look even younger than she was, dressed in the most colorful version of the standard IT uniform I'd ever seen. Vivid purple khakis, I kid you not, and a violet shirt with computer-mouse-shaped buttons that had a fabulous shimmer to it.

But I think her huge grin did the most to transform her whole attitude.

"Well, I figured the least I could do to thank you was get here early enough to supply your brain juice needs." She nearly skipped forward to grab my tankard and Laura's too. "If you'll allow me, I'd love your opinion of my brew."

She danced over to the stainless-steel caffeine goddess, leaving me to stare at Laura open-mouthed.

"I appreciate that, I truly do," I said, demonstrating all my years of knowledge and experience in solving problems. "But I don't understand. Don't you work the evening shift?"

Tia hummed to herself without looking back, filling our tankards with almost the whole pot of steaming hot coffee. When she turned around, I swear the mysterious thrill that got her up and out and bouncy so early in the morning was about to burst out of her and brighten up the whole city.

"I do indeed work evenings. Or I used to. I get the feeling that might be changing soon. Drink, both of you. Then sit."

I'd never claim to be able to resist the command to drink coffee, especially when feeling puny and peaked, and when faced with a brew that carried such a heavenly aroma. So naturally Laura and I did what we were told.

The elixir of intellect somehow managed to taste even better than it smelled, and Laura and I let out embarrassingly matched sighs.

Then Tia proved she'd learned plenty over the weekend about drama and presentation when she made a show of taking a leisurely drink from her brand-new mid-sized Junior Caffeine Tankard before she said a word.

She'd somehow found time to upgrade from her child-sized Newbie model, but sensibly not to the same vast capacity Laura and I guzzled. This was a young woman wise—and aware of her own limits—well beyond her years.

"The truth is I got a text message late last night from the overnight help desk manager. Who's now been promoted to the day shift. She starts next week, mainly to give her time to adjust her sleep schedule. Sounded to me like they more or less *begged* her to start today, but she refused. She also made it clear she had a team in mind to bring to the new shift with her."

Laura nodded and smiled at me, then Tia.

"And you're on the list. As you damn well should be."

Tia blushed and ducked her head, but the joy in her eyes was too lively to hide away that easily.

"I could not agree more that you deserve the first of many promotions," I said, "but you're going to force me to ask the obvious question, aren't you?"

With an eyelash-fluttering "Surely you don't mean sweet, innocent little me?" look, Tia held a hand to her chest.

"You are purely wicked, Tia, and you've learned a couple of lessons *too* well. Fine, I'll do the honors." I fluttered one hand and did my own pearl-clutching impersonation. "But *Tia*, dear, doesn't the help desk already *have* a day-shift manager?"

Now Tia's eyes widened in feigned shock, and she snapped her fingers.

"Why *Angie*, I do believe you're right! No one around the office seems to know exactly why, but it seems our manager resigned over the weekend. Not only that, but he's planning to decamp up to Massachusetts where he came from. Seems he got homesick all of a sudden."

I blinked, caught in one of those moments when you're afraid to react. Because if you're too excited, you seem mean, but if you're not excited enough, you seem ungrateful.

And most of all, in this case, I felt a slithering fear that if I said or did or even thought the wrong thing, this unbelievable news would turn out to be a cruel joke.

I hadn't known Laura all that long, but she once again showed a remarkable ability to say exactly the right thing. And demonstrated why she'd so completely won and warmed my shriveled little heart.

"Good. I'd say he'll keep better in the cold."

Thank the goddess of good timing and not wanting to spew coffee all over Tia's delightful outfit, I had time to swallow before snorting out a most undignified laugh.

"He must have gotten a much better job offer,

huh? Nothing else could explain such an abrupt departure."

"I'm *sure* that's it," Tia said. The sparkle in her eyes gave away the game. "Middle-aged middle managers get great offers including relocation costs all the time, right? And they almost never quit a job midstream without any prospects to replace what they're leaving."

"Someone *will* let us know where he fetches up, right?" I said. "It remains to be seen whether he keeps up with his promises to us or simply starts up his sexist ways in a new part of the country. I hate to admit it, but I feel like a warning would be in order for whoever he ends up working with."

Laura took a long, slow drink of her socially acceptable addictive drug, then tilted her head to the side.

"I think the women who so kindly looked into Mike's background will probably check from time to time. You know, the way people spy on their ex on social media once in a while, then go on about their lives. And Ansi would remind us that a quick, *legal* word to the wise isn't a bad idea, no matter how satisfying it might be to send detailed files to the HR department of every place he interviews with. But if any of us pays too much attention to the not-at-all-dearly departed, we'd be straying into creepy stalker world."

Tia raised her freshly earned Junior Tankard.

"Not to mention wasting our lives and our time on someone who already caused enough misery. He never was worth it, and he sure as hell isn't now."

I'd be lying if I didn't admit to a generous dollop of pride at how our work-child was showing signs of turning out.

"That doesn't mean a bit of a celebration isn't in order," I said. "I'd say Juan would welcome a return engagement of our planning party. With Tia, Edgar and Edie, and all the fabulous guys who stood by us women."

Laura grinned. "Ohhhh, I'd bet Millie and her friends would love it. Either as honored guests, or collaborating with Juan's culinary wizards in the kitchen. Might be some amazing connections for them as a much-deserved benefit."

"I can't believe I'm admitting this," Tia said, "but I'm honestly grateful for my own run-in with Misogynistic Mike. Thank you for interrupting my personal pity party, Angie. And thank you *both* for rescuing me."

For a second, I was worried about tears welling in Tia's eyes. But only until she put down her coffee and grabbed our free hands.

Now I can't believe I'm admitting *this*, but I teared up a little myself. Just like any proud pseudo-parent would when seeing their work-child taking her first steps out into the big, bad world, fully equipped with enough sass and strength to make that world her own personal bitch.

I stand by my original declaration that the break room truly is the beating heart of any good workplace.

But once in a while, if you're lucky, and stubborn enough to last long enough to make it happen, you might find a rare gig where the people rank right up there with the free caffeine.

Thank you for joining the team on the journey to revenge, and satisfaction! We get great things done when we work together, and that's absolutely true for writers and readers.

For more from Kari Kilgore, turn the page or visit www.KariKilgore.com.

NerdyTalesFromKariKilgore.com

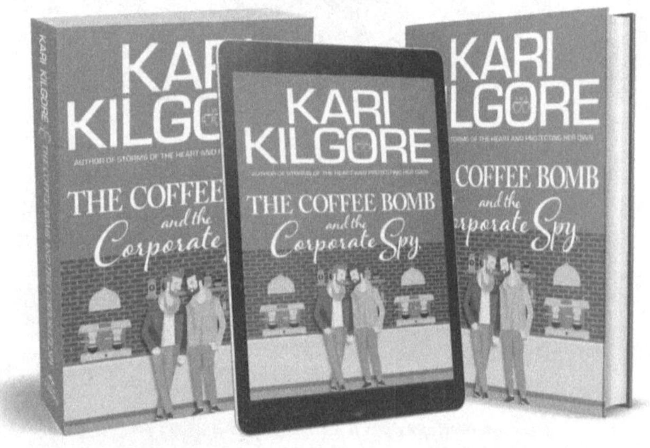

Stories Featuring Hackers and Nerds and Tech, Oh My!

More Nerdy IT-Themed Tales from Kari Kilgore

Always With Jargon at a Managable Mimimum

www.TeamBuildingRevenge.com/
Merch

Team Building
REVENGE
Down o
Senior Caffeine Tankard
TeamBuildingRevenge.com
Newbie Caffeine Tankard
TeamBuildingRevenge.com

Down on the Cube Farm

Meet Your Caffeination Requirements Nerd Style!

ALSO BY KARI KILGORE

I hope you enjoyed reading *Team Building Revenge* as much as I enjoyed writing it.

If you love tales from the nerdy side of life, pay a visit to www.NerdyTalesFromKariKilgore.com. For more stories where speculative elements are slight or not there at all, head over to www.KariKilgore.com/ContemporaryFiction.

For more genre-spanning tales with LGBTQ+ characters, head over to www.KariKilgore.com/LGBTQStories.

Check out more of my fiction, including almost every genre, and be first to hear about release dates, Kickstarters and other fun projects, and exclusive e-book and print editions at www.KariKilgore.com.

Novels:

Until Death

The Dream Thief

Hand Me Downs

Protecting Her Own

The Coffee Bomb and the Corporate Spy

The Great Gold Record Heist

Novellas:

Legacy of the Land

In the Pines

Fantastic Women: A Dark Fantasy Novella Trio

DNA Never Lies

The Box of Possibilities

Murder at the Fabulous Feline Emporium

Dispatches from the Galaxy:

Restricted Species

The Becalmed

Plurapod Pathogen

The Changes Cascade

Near Future Forward (with Jason A. Adams)

Dispatches from the Galaxy: A Space Opera Novella Trio

Dangerous Days on a Pleasure Planet

Storms of Future Past:

Dreaming the Storm

Joining the Storm

Into the Storm

Fighting the Storm

Storms of the Heart

Storms of Future Past Omnibus

Voices Through Time:

Songs in the Mountain

Secrets in the Land

Sorrows in the Earth

Walking the Ghosts

The Odd Society:

Independent by Means of Magic

Protected by Means of Magic

Collections:

Fantastic Shorts: Volume 1

Fantastic Shorts: Volume 2

Fantastic Shorts: Volume 3

Escape into Romance

Stepping Out of Reality

Facing Down Extraordinary

Hacking Cybercrime

Investigations Beyond Belief

Passages in the Real World

Fantastic Side Trips

A Kaleidoscope of Cat Tales

A Tapestry of Holiday Tales

Aunties Among Us

Four-Legged Heroes

Anthologies *with Jason A. Adams:*

Partners in Romance

Shadows Mountain Deep

Uncommon Holidays

Partnership in Crime

ABOUT KARI

Kari Kilgore's wanderlust and imagination lead her all over the world on grand adventures. Her heart and family bring her home to her native Appalachian Mountains of Virginia. From that solid base and with the help of the ever-changing lens of her imagination, she brings those adventures to life in fiction.

She survived her time in the IT trenches with only a few scars to go with countless story seeds, a lingering love/hate relationship with technology, and lifelong dear friends.

Kari writes contemporary fiction, romance, fantasy, mystery, and science fiction, and she's happiest when she surprises herself. She lives with her husband and fellow author Jason A. Adams, various house critters, and wildlife they're better off not knowing more about.

The Confidential Adventure Club

For Kari's exclusive free After The End stories and deleted scenes, discounts, early releases, adorable pet photos, Kickstarters and other fun

projects, Spiral Publishing Exclusive Edition e-books
and print books, and a whole lot more not available
anywhere else, join us in The Club.

Hope to see you there!

www.KariKilgore.com
www.SpiralPublishing.net
www.ConfidentialAdventureClub.com

BB bookbub.com/authors/kari-kilgore

a amazon.com/author/karikilgore

g goodreads.com/karikilgore

f facebook.com/kari.kilgore.1

www.ingramcontent.com/pod-product-compliance
Lightning Source LLC
Chambersburg PA
CBHW050147110726
47898CB00008B/2705